CW00456013

REBEL RAMROD

Texas was Rebel country, full of ex-Confederate ranchers who figured there was nothing wrong with taking the law into their own hands and other ranchers' cattle into their herds. The hired hands closed in on the giant herd from the Big Bend, set for a rustling raid. Conrad Jason had to stop them, even if it meant his own life. He outgunned the hired rustlers, but there was still the big showdown to come...

REBEL RAMROD

Dean Owen

WESTERNS

First published 1960
by Manor Books, Inc.

This hardback edition 1991
by Chivers Press
by arrangement with
Manor Books
in association with
Bobbe Siegel

ISBN 0 86220 992 7

British Library Cataloguing in Publication Data available

Printed and bound in Great Britain by
Redwood Press Limited, Melksham, Wiltshire

Chapter One

IN THE SHADOWED room where he had taken his first breath of air, where his mother had died of the fevers that followed his Texas birth, Conrad Jason explained his reasons for not turning thief. "I don't own Jawbone now," he bluntly told the big dark man who sprawled on a leather sofa pushed against the mud wall. "I only manage it. I won't steal from the men who pay my wages."

Arch Linnbrook jerked upright on the sofa, big hands clenched on his knees. "Since when is it stealin' when you take cows from Yankees?"

Con stood tall in this room that he now used as an office. He leaned against a table littered with the seemingly endless reports he had to file with the Alliance Cattle Company, Chicago. His face was long, brown, his nose a jutting bone. The eyes that watched his lifelong friend were ice-blue under brows bleached almost white from the Texas sun. "Just because we fought them in the war is no sign they're still our enemies. The war's a year done, Arch."

Arch Linnbrook gave a harsh laugh. "An' the Yankees has got Texas under a boot heel." His wide face flushed with anger, Arch got up from the sofa. His big body threw a large shadow across the mud wall. A wedge of sunlight pouring through what Con's father used to call a "gunshot window" touched a scar on his temple. The result of a brawl, Con remembered. But he couldn't recall which one. Con's father had once predicted that because of a long-fused temper that, once it got going, was bad as a Blue Norther, Arch Linnbrook would be dead of a gunshot or rope before he reached eighteen.

Con said, "Nelda's had enough tears because of the war. Don't make it worse and turn rustler on her."

"She'll weep harder if I stay broke." Arch leaned forward. He was more than a hand taller than Con Jason's six feet

5

and heavier by some forty pounds. They were both twenty-five, two days difference in their ages. Arch was the elder. They had grown up together here in the Bend. The war had changed Arch some. But then hadn't the war changed just about everything? Con thought. Nelda was continually reminding him of this fact. Arch went on, "It's for Nelda that I'm doin' this, Con. For her an' for you. An' for me."

"Don't touch a cow on this ranch, Arch. I'm warning you."

"Goddam it! It's one chance in a lifetime! I want you to come in with us!"

"I've told you how I feel about stealing."

Arch strode to the narrow window and looked out onto the yard with its corrals and barn. Con studied the back of Arch's thick neck. It was turning brick-red. He knew well the symptoms. He picked up a gun rig from the littered desk and buckled it around his waist.

Arch said without turning, "You still figure to marry with my sister?"

"It's been planned since the day she was born," Con said, and a tight smile touched the corners of his wide mouth.

"You oughta think of her then."

"Nelda wouldn't want me to turn thief."

Arch's gray eyes got a little red in them. "Nelda's a lady. Some ladies don't mind a little thievin'."

"I'm well aware of that fact, Arch, but it has nothing to do with me turning my back to let you rustle cows from the men I'm sworn to protect—"

"Boy, you got the memory of a short piece of string. We was fightin' them Yankees. Killin' 'em. An' now you say you got to protect 'em."

"Protect their interests is a better way to put it."

Arch wiped a big hand over his mouth, smearing spittle on his chin. "Maybe Pa done wrong sendin' Nelda to that fancy school in Saint Looey. But there's no changin' it now." Arch spat on the dirt floor, took a hitch at his pants. "It'll take a sight more money to keep my sister happy than you'll earn from them Yankee bosses in Chicago."

"Nelda understands my problem," Con said, his face stiff.

"Yeah? Last time you was over she cried half the night." Arch looked exasperated. Con noted the beginnings of the old lethal temper he remembered from boyhood. "Let me put it to you again. Eight or nine thousand head of beef, Con. We push 'em across the river an' this Mex will pay in gold."

"I told you. I'm not a thief."

Arch went on as if he hadn't heard. Sweat glistened on the high forehead. "When it's over we can live in Chihuahua City like *ricos*."

"Listen to me, Arch. Stay away from Jawbone cows!"

"You're purely a damn fool not to jump at this chance, Con," Arch said, his heavy voice shaking now.

"I've been a damn fool in more ways than one," Con said shortly. He was tired of arguing with Arch. They'd been at it for the better part of an hour. Roundup had been finished yesterday and Con felt as if he still breathed a ton of Big Bend dust into his lungs, had sixteen hours a day of jolting saddle under him. The click of cow horns, the stench of burned hair, the smell of heat from branding fires. "I was mostly a damn fool not to stay home from the war and run Jawbone." He looked Arch in the eye. "Maybe then your father wouldn't have sold me out."

Arch flinched. "Pa done wrong. I told him that before he died. But you got to understand he had them notes on Jawbone that your own pa signed. And when he got a chance to sell—"

"Arch, I'm dead for sleep. There's no use arguing about this rustling. I won't throw in with you."

Arch's eyes turned ugly. "You think them Chicago boys give a damn what happens to you?"

"Probably not much. But I've got a conscience."

"You're comin' in with me an' my friends, Con!" Arch shouted.

"What friends?"

"Never mind. You *got* to come in. Maybe I ain't put it straight so you could understand. But there's a storm blowin' up down here. I'm tryin' to keep you from bein' caught up in it, Con."

"You mean if I don't come in, your friends will try and kill me?"

"I don't want you dead. I've knowed you all my life, Con. You're fixin' to marry with my sister—"

"I survived the war," Con said coldly. "I'll survive your friends."

And suddenly Arch's temper spilled over. Without warning, he came swiftly across the dirt floor, big fists swinging. "You got no sense, Con," he almost sobbed. "I'll beat some into you."

But Con backed swiftly and drew his gun. "Last time we fought I was fourteen. You beat the hell out of me. I vowed then it would never happen again. Don't even try to touch me, Arch. I mean it."

Arch had halted abruptly. He stared down at the cocked revolver. Then he lifted his gray eyes to Con's face. Some of the heat had gone out of his eyes. "Listen, boy," Arch said in his heavy voice, "you're the only friend I got in these parts. I want you on my side of the creek when this thing busts open."

"There's no law that says you *have* to turn rustler," Con said. "Turn your back on your friends. You've got a ranch of your own to run."

"I got range but damn few cows," Arch said bitterly. "I want you an' me an' Nelda to have somethin', Con. We deserve it."

"A man earns what he gets. Otherwise it's not worth a frayed rope."

"You're sick of workin' for Jawbone, Con," Arch said, trying again. "You're always writin' them damn reports." He waved a big hand at the papers on the table. "You ain't a cowman no more. You're a goddam pen-pusher."

"Well, part of that will be taken care of. Alliance sent me a clerk last week to help out."

"They also sent you a new *segundo*." Arch, seeing the set of Con's mouth, grinned. "You didn't like it much when they told you this fella Jud Kilhaven is the new *segundo* and you got to demote Charlie Baston. Charlie's just a cowhand now. Kind of sticks under your blanket, don't it, Con? Havin' to set down a fella like Charlie Baston. Hell, he come here with your pa way back before we fought with Mexico—"

"Arch, I don't like working for Alliance worth a damn." Con felt his voice shake and cursed himself for lack of control. "But it's all I have. In a year I'll have a herd built.

I'm taking most of my wages in cows. I'll pick out land and then I'll get married."

"You think over what I been tellin' you, Con," Arch said. His gaze flicked again to the revolver in Con's hand. "Hope you get some sense. I'd feel poor as hell if you an' me ended up swappin' lead."

"This talk of thieving. It's something new with you, Arch. Just since the war."

Arch's face flushed and his eyes had that dangerous look again. "You talkin' about last year?"

"I'm not accusing you, Arch," Con said steadily. "But there has been some talk. You took a pool herd north."

"An' I lost it. To Comanches!"

"In Missouri?"

"They get that far east sometimes." Arch's hair was the color of water sluiced over rusted iron. He grabbed his hat off the leather sofa. He set the hat straight on his head. "You remember this, Con. You an' me been friends all our lives. We're closer than you ever was to your brother, Big Ed. You an' me is 'milk brothers' my ma used to say."

Con swallowed something gritty and looked away. One fact he could not deny. Arch Linnbrook's mother had given him life. Con looked around this room. If it hadn't been for Mrs. Linnbrook he would never have left these four walls. He would have died soon after his mother had breathed her last—

Con holstered the gun. The Linnbrooks had given him so much. They had taken so much. Mrs. Linnbrook giving him his life. Bert Linnbrook, her husband, selling him out. On the other hand there was Nelda, giving. And Arch wanting to take. Take his decency. Begging him to turn thief.

"Charlie Baston's howling to get in a poker game," Con said. "Meet us in Slager's in a few days. I'll let you know." Anything to shut Arch up on the subject of rustling.

Arch regarded him thinly. "When you comin' over to court my sister?"

"Soon as I clear up some reports." He nodded at the table with its papers.

"You got time for poker. You ain't got time for Nelda."

"I thought it might be better to let her cool down for a change," Con said. "We had some words. She suddenly

decided she wants to live in Denver. Wants me to take a job
there. Guess you know what my answer was to that, Arch."

"You're as mule-headed as your pa was about the war."
Arch went to the door. "See you in a few days."

"Be careful, Arch," Con said softly.

Arch looked back. "You warnin' me?"

"You've been seen along the river with some hardcases.
Just don't get your neck tangled up in somebody's rope."

"Your rope?"

"You know better than that, Arch."

When Arch Linnbrook had gone, Con poured himself a
stiff drink of whisky. Something he rarely did during the
day, unless it was at Slager's Saloon in Santa Margarita.

He went outside and stared south where the Chisos Mountains climbed into the clear sky. Down there in that rough
country he would build his life, starting with the cows he
was taking as payment for being foreman-manager of Jawbone. Or what the Alliance Cattle Company called Number
Three. They owned two other cattle ranches, these in New
Mexico.

Con went down to the lean-to built against the end of
the bunkhouse. Homer Peale, the new clerk, was making out
a report. He looked around, his pale eyes watching Con.
Peale was of medium height, his small face framed by tight
red curls.

Con made no attempt to hide his dislike. He asked Peale
what he was doing.

"Filling out a report," Peale said, "on the new harness
we had to buy." He nodded at the sheet of paper on the
desk. Despite the heat he wore a dark sack coat. His right
arm, resting on the desk, tightened the coat sleeve so that
it revealed the outline of some hard object. A derringer, Con
knew. It wasn't the first time he had noticed this. He wondered if Homer Peale thought he was fooling anybody.

In addition to the derringer, Peale wore an ivory-butted
revolver shoved into the waistband of his trousers.

Peale said, "You got the tally on the calf crop yet?"

"I'll figure it out tonight," Con said, looking around. Although he used a former bedroom at the house for his own
office, he told Peale to work down here. Peale and the new

segundo, Jud Kilhaven, had arrived together. And they could bunk together.

A sheet of paper tacked to a wall plank caught his eye. He walked over. It was the order Kilhaven had brought with him. It informed Con Jason that Kilhaven was to be the new *segundo.* The company felt that Charlie Baston, the present *segundo,* was too old for such a responsible position. The order was signed by Bentley Hake, one of the partners in Alliance. He was in charge of operations.

Con jerked the paper from the wall, went over and put it on the table Peale used for a desk. "No need for Kilhaven to keep this posted," Con said coldly, staring down into Peale's pale eyes. "I know the orders."

"Wasn't my doin'," Peale said.

Con started for the door, then looked around. "Kind of a warm day for wearing a coat."

"Don't bother me none."

"You always wear a derringer?"

Peale's gaze did not change. "I've worked in some rough places. Force of habit, I guess."

Con went out, wondering how long it would take Bentley Hake to answer his letter. He had told Hake that he was not impressed with either Homer Peale or Jud Kilhaven. And the first time either of them gave him trouble, they were through.

He had also written Hake about Charlie Baston.

And Charlie Baston was now coming out of the bunkhouse, scratching himself. His mustache looked like a piece of down-curving dirty rope. It was as gray as the hair at his temples. His face was flushed and he walked unevenly and Con knew that Baston's semi-annual drunk was getting a fair start already. And roundup only over yesterday.

"Let's take a ride, Charlie," Con said.

"Hell, I figure to play me some poker at Slager's."

"Your money will keep. I want to talk to you."

They rode south, past huisache and sotol, flushing quail from mesquite. Con said, "I want you to know that you're still carried on the books as *segundo.*"

"I'm nothin' but a goddam cowhand," Charlie Baston said, and took a pull from a bottle he carried in his saddlebag. The whisky spilled onto the ends of his mustache and down the front of his shirt.

"They're paying you *segundo* wages," Con said. "Alliance may give me orders about a lot of things, but when it comes to my men—especially the old-timers like you—they don't rope me too tight."

Baston corked the bottle, turned his small, bloodshot eyes on Con. "Them bastard Yankees. I hate ever' goddam one of 'em."

"They pay our wages," Con said stiffly.

"Mule shidd." Charlie Baston rubbed a hand over the mutilated lobe of his right ear, the long saber slash below it on his neck. "They're tryin' to get rid of you. Can't you see that, Con?"

"No. I can't see it."

"They send Kilhaven an' Peale. Them two is mean as a gut-shot grizzly."

"They make one wrong move and they're through."

"You won't be doin' much firin', Con," Charlie Baston said soberly, "if we got you buried out back of the barn."

"It's one thing I wanted to talk to you about. Help me keep an eye on them, Charlie."

They rode in silence for several miles, the dust ballooning up from their horses. At last Charlie Baston said bitterly, "Maybe it's a good thing your Poppa an' Big Ed never come back from the war. They'd be some sick to see Jawbone owned by blue-bellies in Chicago."

"I don't exactly like it myself, Charlie."

"Then why in the hell didn't you fight for it?" the older man demanded. "Fight for Jawbone. Your poppa would've done it. And so would your brother. Alliance Cattle Company—"

"They bought Jawbone legally. I had nothing to say—"

"We shoot Yankees for four years. An' then just because they trick Lee into givin' up his sword, we're s'posed to lick the mud off their boots."

Con started to say something, then broke off. He remembered all too well the day Leroy Marcom, ex-major of the Union forces, sat with him at a corner table in Slager's Saloon. And with Marcom was a lawyer. And they had legal documents and a court order. Con no longer owned Jawbone.

"We want you to run Jawbone for us," Marcom had said. "You're highly recommended."

It was two days before he could give Marcom his answer. He agreed. But only on the stipulation that he receive most of his wages in cattle.

Now Charlie Baston said, after taking another drink, "If it was me, I'd make a fort outa Jawbone an' tell them Yankees to close hell's door after 'em on the way down."

"They bought Jawbone through due process of law—"

"An' if that didn't work, I'd run off ever' damn head of beef and sell it somewheres."

Con jerked around in the saddle, studying the harsh profile of this man who had taught him to ride, to shoot. Taught him the things a boy should know. His own father had always been too busy for these things.

Con said softly, "Have you been talking to Arch Linnbrook?"

"That son—" Charlie Baston made a savage swipe at his saddle horn, the sudden movement of his hand causing his horse to rear. When Baston got it quieted, he said, "I got no use for Arch. Never did have, so far as that goes."

"Arch changed with the war."

"He never was no damn good. Why, way back him an' your brother chasin' them Mex gals into the brush—" Baston broke off. "Never should've said that, Con."

"Go ahead. Finish it. Say that it was Poppa who gave them the idea. Great sport, Poppa said." Con's mouth was bitter.

"Only Mex your poppa ever had use for was Timoteo."

"Timoteo's as white a man as any who ever lived."

"Reckon." Baston splattered a sotol bush with tobacco juice. "I recollect like it was yesterday old Timoteo puttin' you under his coat. An' it rainin' like God had a big bucket up yonder. An' you wrapped in a serape. By God, you wasn't no bigger'n the nose of this here roan I'm ridin'. An' your own ma layin' there dead—" Baston scowled down at the dusty trail they were following. "All the way to the Linnbrook place old Timoteo carried you. An' Missus Linnbrook givin' one nipple to her boy Arch. An' one to you."

"Milk brothers, she used to say we were."

"Timoteo carryin' you way over there instead of your

poppa doin' it." Baston's scowl was black and he gave a vicious jerk to the end of his mustache.

Con said, "Don't worry, Charlie. I know what Poppa was doing the night I was born."

"Never could rightly figure your poppa out, Con."

"He told me later it made him nervous to be around a woman about to throw a foal." Con gave a harsh laugh. "I guess that's all I ever was to Poppa. A foal."

"He had a heart as hard as the grapeshot that killed him. But one thing for sure, if Yankees had tried to jerk Jawbone out from under him"—Baston gave Con a sour grin—"there'd be a passel of dead Yankees."

"We've got to abide by the due process of law. It's all we have left."

"Some folks was a mite surprised you never fought them Yankees off."

"I know." Con sighed, remembering the looks he got these days when he went to Santa Margarita. And none of his old neighbors ever dropped by any more.

"Had you given the word, Con," Charlie Baston said gravely, "ever' man in this corner of Texas would've come to Jawbone an' helped you stand off them blue-bellies."

"And the weeping widows would have been my responsibility." Con shook his head. "And in the end the new owners would have taken over anyway."

"That's like what folks told your poppa," Charlie Baston said, "when he was fixin' to come out here in the Thirties. They said, 'You'll never live a year. The Comanches will kill you dead. An' if you don't think of your own hide, you oughta think of that purty wife of yours.'" Baston turned in the saddle. "An' your ma was purty, Con. Her an' your poppa built a ranch here. They fought off ever' damn thing, red an' white from both sides of the line. I helped 'em do it, an' so did Timoteo an' some of the others that is gone now."

"I'm aware of all that," Con said stiffly. "You and Timoteo will have jobs as long as I live—"

"You're in a trap, son," Baston said, his voice sober. "You feel you owe somethin' to me an' the old Mex. But on one side you got Alliance. Them Yankees say me an' Timoteo are too damn old. They want to send in their own men."

"Over my dead body."

"And that might happen." Baston spat again. "Don't turn your back on Peale an' Kilhaven."

"I don't intend to." Con looked ahead at the mountains. He saw the dust cloud where his men were pushing a thousand head of beef into the Chisos for summer graze. There was roughly another seven thousand head of Jawbone cattle scattered over a fifty-mile area.

At last they came within sight of the herd spreading across a mesa. His ten-man crew—not counting Kilhaven—looked pitifully small. He'd written Alliance about being short-handed, but they told him the crew was sufficient, especially as long as no cattle drive to northern markets would be made this year. Bentley Hake, who seemed to be the cattle expert for Alliance, had written that he thought it better to let the northern beef market improve before pushing a herd over the trail. Next year they'd go north, Hake had written.

Con said, "Another point I wanted to bring up, Charlie. I may have trouble with Arch." He briefly sketched Arch Linnbrook's proposal. "Don't spread it around. Just keep your eyes open."

"Arch is fixin' to get himself hung to a tree. Wonder it didn't happen last year when he lost that pool herd."

"Everybody's a little afraid of Arch."

"I was in Slager's last week an' I heard Billy Snider an' Millot an' some of them other raggedy-pants boys tellin' what they'd do if they ever catched Arch out alone. Each one of them boys lost a hundred head of cows in that deal."

"They like to talk a lot."

"You'll be Arch's brother-in-law one of these days," Baston said. "Be tough if some of them old neighbors of yours kill him." And when Con said nothing, Baston squinted at him. "You still figure to marry with Nelda?"

"When I get a herd built."

It was then that the dust kicked up by the cows cleared a little, thinning against the cliffs. Con saw his riders bunched. The cattle were grazing, paying no attention to the man who lay on the ground. The man had lost his hat. Dust powdered his gray-streaked black hair. And on one dark cheek there was a stain of blood.

"Timoteo," Con said through his teeth, and drew his gun.

And in that moment he set spurs against his dun. A sudden sob burst from Charlie Baston, followed by the crack of a rifle. Turning his head, Con saw Baston nearly fall, right himself in the saddle. Through the fingers gripping his right shoulder was a steady pulsing redness.

Chapter Two

HOLSTERING HIS REVOLVER, Con jerked free his rifle, and shouted at Charlie Baston to hang on. Then he yelled for some of his men to follow him. The rest were to stay behind with Baston and Timoteo. Con sent his dun racing for a ridge, because from the sound of the rifle shot that was where the ambusher had been hiding. But when they reached there they found nothing. Only a shell case, a cigarette still smoking under a heel print, and the tracks of a man and then of a horse. The tracks moving north.

Con swallowed and turned to Jake Deward, who had swung down beside him to study the sign. "Timoteo. Is he bad hurt?"

"Kilhaven beefed him with his gun barrel." The black-bearded rider wore a dusty patch over his left eye.

"Where's Kilhaven now?"

"Said he was headin' for home to palaver with you," Deward said thinly. "Said we was all fired."

"Oh, he did, did he?" Con was staring northward where a thin streamer of dust was moving swiftly.

"Reckon Kilhaven hung around long enough to shoot Charlie," Jake Deward said. "I seen him headin' up this way just before you come."

"He better brush up on his rifle shooting."

"It's for sure he got Charlie."

"It's for sure he was aiming at me."

Deward wanted to ride after Kilhaven, but Con said it was a personal matter, to be handled by one Con Jason. White-faced, he rode back to the mesa. The cattle had moved off to the south end where the grass was thicker. A hawk soared on stiffened wings. The sun burned through the back of Con's shirt.

Timoteo was sitting up, supported by Dave Rubel, the round-faced kid who usually laughed a lot. Rubel wasn't laughing now. The front of Timoteo's shirt was stained with blood. The thin-faced old Mexican looked gray around the mouth.

"Ai, Chico," Timoteo murmured, using the term of affection from Con's boyhood. "Somebody hit me with an anvil, no?" He fingered his gashed cheek. "Señor Kilhaven do this."

"I'll take care of him," Con said roughly. He walked over to where Charlie Baston stood. Sam Trench, long in the arm and leg, built like an awning post, was binding up Baston's shoulder with pieces torn from an old shirt.

"Charlie, you get for town. Doc Maxfield will fix you up." Con said, "Sam, you go with him."

"I can go alone," Baston grunted, his voice thick with pain. He glanced toward the ridge where the ambusher had been holed up. "I'll kill him."

"I'll do it for you, if necessary," Con said coldly. "You do what I tell you. Get for town. And quit that drinking till Doc—"

Baston reeled over to his horse. Sam Trench tried to help him into the saddle, but Baston kicked him away. He moved north, in the direction taken by the streamer of dust.

"Kilhaven will finish him," Deward said, a little worriedly. "Charlie ain't in no shape for a fight."

"I'll catch up with him. Jake, what happened here, anyway?"

Deward said that they had just reached the mesa when Kilhaven, who had been riding them hard all day, said they were to push the herd ten miles south to Caballo Canyon. "It's where you got your own herd bunched, Con," Deward said. "We knowed you don't want Jawbone cows mixed up with yours. At least until you make a calf count—"

"I tell him this, Chico." Timoteo said, coming up. He held a bandanna to his bleeding face. His dark eyes looked sick.

"And then he hit you," Con finished, and felt such a murderous rage sweep him that his body shook. He wondered then whether living for so long in Arch Linnbrook's shadow had made him assume some of the man's lethal temper. At the moment he would gladly have hung Kilhaven by his heels over hot coals, as the Comanches used to do . . . until a man's skull popped open like a melon.

"We'd have jumped him," Deward said glumly, "but he had us covered."

"He's hell on a greased pole with that gun of his," Sam Trench put in. "I never liked that son from the day he showed up here. You watch out for him, Con."

Con put a hand on Timoteo's thin arm. "Can vou ride, old man?" he asked in Spanish.

Timoteo nodded, his teeth clenched in pain.

Without another word Con mounted and spurred his dun in the direction taken by Charlie Baston. Within a mile he caught up with him. Baston was riding at a jog and even this jolting evidently tore at the wounded shoulder.

"You take the town road," Con ordered.

"I'm goin' after him myself."

"You're going to obey orders for once in your life," Con snapped.

Baston slanted his gaze at him. "Reckon you know he was shootin' at you. I pulled my hoss up just when he cut loose."

"He won't be around to shoot anybody else."

"You figure to kill him?"

"If he wants it. But first I'm going to beat the hell out of him."

"He come here for one reason, Con. To kill you. I had a hunch about it. Him an' that Peale."

"You do what I tell you." But Baston tried to argue. At last Con had his word that he would go to town and let the doctor treat his arm.

"Don't go after Kilhaven by yourself, Con. Wait for the boys to catch up."

Con sat in his saddle, staring at this land his father had claimed so long ago. He was remembering his father's story of how Charlie Baston had given the ranch its name. Originally it had been called the Lazy J, but the first branding iron was poorly designed, and with the shank too long and the hook at the end too narrow Charlie Baston said one day that it looked more like the jawbone of a bull than a "J" for Jason.

Con said, "Kilhaven is my problem, Charlie. Mine alone."

He rode off before Baston could say anything more. He didn't want Charlie Baston to get mixed up in any showdown. The man was getting old, a fact he wouldn't admit. He would be no match for the pair Alliance had sent here last week. Even sober he would be no match.

As he rode toward Jawbone headquarters, he thought, Maybe I'm wrong. Maybe I should have fought for Jawbone, and when Marcom and his lawyer came with their papers, I should have shown them a gun. Instead of signing my name to a contract. Did the war really change everything? As Nelda claims? As Arch claims? Are the old moral values no longer valid?

But he shook off the thoughts that were pounding through his head. No, the old moral values were not dead. But he did feel responsible for Kilhaven's being on Jawbone. When the man first arrived with Peale and showed his orders from Bentley Hake, Con had a premonition of disaster. Maybe that was when he should have made his stand. Torn up Hake's orders and written Chicago that he was not taking on the pair that Alliance had sent. True, he had sent a letter of protest, but he probably would not receive an answer until summer. It was the frustrating way things usually worked out.

He came in on headquarters by circling far to the west. Leaving his horse in the cottonwood grove that had been planted by his father, he crept up to the lean-to. At first he thought the whole headquarters area was deserted. Even the cook, Sam Trench, put in time at saddlework these days. Thanks to Alliance making him run with a short crew, Con thought bitterly.

Then as he pressed his ear against the lean-to wall he heard Kilhaven mutter, "The damn Mex—"

Con went around to the front door and walked in. Peale was still sitting at the desk. His fingertips were stained with ink. He looked around, brushing a lock of curly red hair away from his forehead. Kilhaven was sitting on the edge of a cot, a whisky bottle between his bony knees.

"You come up some quiet," Kilhaven drawled.

"It's the Comanche in me," Con said coldly.

Without taking his eyes from Kilhaven, Con suddenly grabbed Peale by the back of his sack coat, ripping it. He hauled Peale out of the chair. He held the squealing Peale in front of him as a shield while Kilhaven just stood there, his muddy-brown eyes narrowed. The black handle of his gun jutted out from a narrow hip.

Still watching Kilhaven, Con jerked up the sleeve of Peale's coat, revealing a derringer. Con ripped the weapon free, tearing one of the straps from the sleeve holster. He threw the derringer over his shoulder into the yard. He then hauled up the ivory-butted gun from Peale's waistband. With an underhand toss he sent it back through the doorway. Then he pushed Peale over against the desk.

"You're a rotten shot, Kilhaven," Con said.

Kilhaven said, "The Mex give me an argument. I figured he was goin' to draw on me, so I laid my gun barrel on his face. You rather I'd shot him?"

"You shot Charlie Baston. That's enough for one day."

Kilhaven took a step forward. He moved lazily. He spoke the same way. He wore a dirty flat-crowned hat on the back of his head. His hair was long, curling down the back of his neck, around his ears and down either side of his narrow face. He had high cheekbones and a jutting jaw. He brushed his hair back, careful to keep both hands well above his belt line. Then he set his hat squarely on his head.

"You been drinkin, Jason," he said lazily, "if you say I shot Charlie Baston. Hell, I ain't laid my poor eyes on that boy since yesterday."

"You saw me coming with Baston. You hung around, up on the ridge above the mesa. You fired at me, but Baston got in the way."

Kilhaven looked pained. "You ain't been drinkin'. You been smokin' a Chinese pipe to say a thing like that. Why would I want to shoot at you?"

"I'll likely have the answer to that after I drag your face through the yard dirt a few times."

"You're bigger'n me," Kilhaven drawled. "Ain't he, Homer?" He turned his muddy eyes on Peale. The clerk hung against the front of the desk where Con had pushed him. His face was white. His torn coat was off one shoulder. A holster strap dangled from his wrist.

"Wouldn't be fair for you to beat up on me," Kilhaven drawled. But there was an edge of worry in his eyes now.

"It might be quicker and cleaner to put a bullet in you. It's your move, Kilhaven."

The man gave a slight shrug with his bony shoulders. "You better be careful how you take on, Jason. Bentley Hake is a friend of mine—"

"I've written Hake. If we had the telegraph in this part of the country I'd damn soon let Hake know how things stand here."

"You better watch out," Kilhaven said calmly, "or you'll go gittin' yourself fired."

Keeping an eye on Peale, Con edged around so he stood within three feet of Kilhaven. "You and Peale are the ones fired. Peale, get out of here. I've got a little business to settle with your friend."

"Just because I hit the Mex."

"And shot Charlie Baston."

"Hell, I never shot that boy." Kilhaven spread his hands.

"I found your sign up on the ridge."

"Wasn't my sign," Kilhaven said stoutly. "Must've been one of them boys I been seein' along the river."

"You haven't told me about seeing any boys along the river."

"Hell, you already know about it. Arch said—" Kilhaven, his face flaming, broke off.

Con whipped out, "Go ahead. Finish it. Arch said what?"

Kilhaven just looked at him. The flush still stained his cheeks. It was very quiet in the lean-to. Homer Peale's ragged breathing was the only sound.

Con shifted his gaze slightly to the curly-haired clerk. "Peale, I told you to get out. I won't tell you again."

Peale moved to the door in his torn coat, the strap of the sleeve holster dangling from an arm.

Con looked around at Kilhaven again. "I didn't know you and Arch Linnbrook were acquainted," he said in an icy voice.

"Seen him in town last week. We're neighbors, ain't we?" Kilhaven shrugged as if the matter were of no importance. He started to make a lazy turn as if to go across the room.

And in that moment, when his right side was partially hidden from Con, he reached for his gun.

Con had been watching the man's eyes and when they tightened from pressure, he lunged. He caught Jud Kilhaven half-turned. Crashing into Kilhaven, he knocked the gun loose. It went skating across the dirt floor.

With a forearm at the throat, Con pinned him against the wall. "I want some truth out of you," he grunted, his eyes boring into the other man's face. "And I can't get it if you're dead."

By a sudden twist of his long body Kilhaven managed to squirm away. Desperately he tried to reach his gun. Con caught him by his long hair, jerked him back. They wrestled across the room and Con was aware of the other man's power. He felt it in the straining muscles. They crashed into a table, spilling papers. Before Kilhaven could slip away again Con got him by the throat. A vein throbbed at Kilhaven's temple.

"Talk!" Con cried. "What about you and Arch?"

"I—I knew him in the war. In Missouri. You're chokin' me—"

"Arch never told me. Why didn't Arch tell me he knew you?"

And suddenly Kilhaven twisted away, shouting, "Peale! Get him!"

Con felt the muscles of his back drawn into an aching tautness as he heard the snick-snick of a gun coming to full cock behind him. With his boot heels digging into the dirt floor, Con spun. In that moment he glimpsed Peale hunched over a stack of papers on the table where a .45 had evidently been hidden. Sweating, Peale swung the gun to cover him.

Con reached for his own weapon, felt Kilhaven's hand there. They struggled for possession of the revolver while Peale shouted, "Jud, get away from him!"

A tremendous, jolting right caught Kilhaven on the side of the head. As the *segundo* fell away, Con's gun went with him. With a desperate lunge Con tried to recover the weapon. But he didn't quite make it. He felt the lash of powder flame against his side as Peale fired. Concussion rattled the walls, brought sunlight lancing through a fresh bullet hole in the wall.

Groggy from the blow to the head. Kilhaven was trying to get up. And he held Con's gun. But Con was whipping his long frame around, fists wide from his body like the arms of a steam-engine regulator. One of his looping fists crashed into Kilhaven's skull, knocking him down. The gun went flying, out of reach.

For the moment Peale had been forced to hold his fire for fear of hitting Kilhaven. But now Kilhaven was out of the line of fire. He dropped the gun hammer again, but Con was moving. Con dove head first across Kilhaven's body, and swept the fallen gun into his hand.

On his knees, he turned. Peale was backing out the door, his face tight. To Con the .45 in Peale's hand looked big as the cannon they said his father and brother, Big Ed, had foolishly charged with flashing sabers during the last disorganized stand of the war.

And it was the things Con himself had learned in the war that saved his life. Peale was rattled and he fired again, but Con had thrown himself flat. The bullet went screaming over his head. He fired once into the thickest part of Peale's body. The heavy slug drove the clerk backward out the door as if shouldered down by a runaway horse.

Turning, Con lined his weapon on Kilhaven. The Chicago-appointed *segundo* was on hands and knees, long hair framing his face. His hat was on his back, hanging from a chin strap that dug into the thin brown throat. Kilhaven had been reaching for his gun, which lay against the dirt. He jerked his hand back as if he had touched hot metal. Slowly he got to his feet, his eyes murderous. His gaze swung to the yard where Peale lay on his side.

"If he's dead," Jud Kilhaven said, breathing heavily, "you're through at Jawbone."

"You've got it wrong. You're the one through here."

At the point of a gun he herded Kilhaven into the yard. He looked down at Peale. The man had his two hands pressed against the wound just above the buckle of his belt. Peale's eyes were open, staring. His short legs made running movements. And dust clouded up as his feet dragged across

the dirt. In a moment they were stilled and Peale's hands
fell away loosely.

Chapter Three

THERE WAS A sudden rattle of wagon wheels, the sound of
hoofs. "Get over by the wall," Con ordered Kilhaven. The
man, still with hands lifted, did as he was told.

In a few moments a wagon with *88* burned in its side
came wheeling around the house. It was driven by one of
Arch Linnbrook's men, Joe Leacham. Three other 88 hands
were in the saddle. Sharing the narrow wagon seat with
Leacham was Nelda Linnbrook, wearing a green silk dress
that matched the color of her eyes. On her pinned-up dark-
red hair she wore a bonnet with a green feather in it.

The cavalcade came slowly down the yard and halted.
Nobody said anything. The four 88 men nodded at Con. They
stared at Kilhaven, backed against the wall with his hands up.
Then they looked at Peale crumpled on the ground. Already
a mat of green flies was at the wound.

Nelda, a hand over her full-lipped mouth, closed her
eyes. "Oh, my God," she whispered. "The war all over
again." Con could see her dark lashes, see the paleness
around the nostrils. "Did you kill him, Con?" she asked
hoarsely.

He nodded tiredly. "This was a bad time for you to
come, Nelda." She said nothing to this. She sat there, clenching, unclenching her pale hands. Con looked at the 88 men
in their sweat-marked hats, their dusty clothes. Each man
with a belt gun and a booted rifle. And Joe Leacham with
a rifle on the floorboards of the wagon.

Con said, nodding at Kilhaven, "Any of you boys know
him?" The former *segundo* stood stiffly. One side of his
face was swelling from Con's fist.

The 88 men looked him over and shook their heads.
But Leacham said, "Seen him in town a time or two, Con."

Con jerked his gun barrel at Kilhaven. "You came here
with one horse. You leave with one. If you ever set foot

on Jawbone again I'll personally hang you. And if you ever touch Timoteo again you'll wish I'd only hanged you."

Kilhaven ran a tongue over his lips, glanced at the 88 men and then walked down to the nearest corral. Nobody said anything until he had roped out his personal horse and ridden out. Then Con felt the tension drain out of him. He holstered his gun. Sunlight winked on Peale's .45, his derringer lying in the yard.

Leacham, elbows on his knees, had been holding the team in because the scent of blood made them nervous. As it did the three saddlers. Leacham said, nodding at Peale's body, "Reckon you don't figure to pack him clear to the sheriff."

"Ninety miles in this heat and they'd smell him clear to Mexico City," Con said.

"One thing about not havin' law no closer then San Pablo," Leacham observed. "A man can usually do his own buryin' without answerin' a lot of fool questions."

"Guess I'd better get him under the ground," Con said tiredly. The weeks of roundup, the strain of trying to run a ranch the size of Jawbone was wearing him thin.

Nelda straightened her bonnet. "You boys bury him," she said to her brother's men. "I want to talk to Con."

The men said nothing. Leacham swung down. He was in his forties, but had a face seamed and weathered so that it looked almost half again as old. Texas did that to a man, he often said. He had been at 88 since Arch was a boy. "Reckon you keep the shovels in the same old place," he grunted at Con and handed him the reins. Con climbed into the wagon.

"Thanks, boys," he said. "I'll do the same for you one day."

"Got a feelin' we'll all be in practice diggin' graves before long," Leacham observed. Con felt Nelda shudder beside him on the wagon seat. The other three 88 hands tied their horses. Two of them carried Peale's body down behind the barn.

Con drove down to the willows that lined Kentucky Creek. The old man had named the creek for Con's mother.

On the cool grass, with the team tied close by, Nelda sat with her hands in her lap. "You couldn't come over to see me," she said petulantly. "So I came to see you."

"Running a ranch for absentee owners isn't the same as

running it for yourself," he said with a shake of his head. "The paper work—"

"I'm not interested in anything but you." Leaning over she pressed her mouth against his cheek. She drew back and said, "You're disgusted with Jawbone."

"I don't like having to kill a man."

"He probably deserved it," she said, and unpinned her bonnet and put it on the grass beside her.

"It was either he kill me or I kill him. Yes, I'd say his death was deserved. But you seem to take it lightly enough."

"Don't be angry."

"I didn't like Peale alive. I don't like him any better now. But he was a human being. I—I just can't dismiss it as casually as you do."

"I saw the wounded brought into St. Louis during the war. I guess I got used to death. Insulated against it would be a better way to put it."

"Arch was over today," he said, watching her from the corners of his eyes.

"I haven't seen him today." Her green gaze touched him. The scent of lavender water was strong about her. It stirred him. "Arch was gone by the time I got up this morning," she went on. "What did he want?"

"A proposition. Do you know about it?"

She looked bitter. "Arch never tells me anything. What sort of proposition?"

"Nothing important." As long as she didn't know about it he had no intention of telling her how Arch planned to turn rustler. Hugging his knees, he studied her. For years they had said in the Bend that Nelda Linnbrook was the prettiest female between Paso del Norte and Austin. She stirred restlessly on the grass and he saw the movement of her body beneath the green silk. He frowned, not liking at all what he knew to be fact.

She said, "When are we going to get married?"

"As I told you last time, honey. I need another year."

"Am I going to lie awake each night for another year?"

"How were the nights in St. Louis when I was fighting a war?"

She glanced down at her lap and plucked a grass stem and put it in her mouth. "That was before you made a woman out of me. I had no reason for sleepless nights then."

"Sometimes I'm not very proud of myself."

"It doesn't bother my conscience. Why should it bother yours? I just need you with more frequency than we are able to manage under present circumstances—"

"You put it so goddam blunt." He grabbed a handful of grass and looked at it and let it fall upon his knees. He got control of his voice. "I'm sorry, but I always thought— Well, that there should be something special about a thing like this."

"It's special, believe me," she whispered, leaning her head against his shoulder. Sunlight drew sparks from the creek. In the distance he saw his men ride in from the Chisos. Timoteo holding a bandanna to his cheek. Charlie Baston was not with them. Good. Then Charlie has obeyed orders and gone to town to get his wound dressed.

When the men passed beyond the trees and entered the ranch yard, Nelda said, "Arch is going to get married."

Con looked around, unable to keep his surprise from showing. Nelda was smoothing the heavy pleats of the green dress. "Arch didn't tell me," Con said.

"I guess he's embarrassed. He's never had much to do with women except the— You know the kind out back of Slager's."

"This is getting to be an earthy conversation," he said. "You didn't talk like this before the war."

"The discussions at Miss Armstead's Academy For Young Ladies weren't always of the arts." She gave a small laugh and then broke off when she saw the annoyance in his face. Her strong teeth were sunk into her lower lip. "I'm sorry, Con, if you think me bold. But girls are interested in such things, you know."

"It's that fancy school that's changed you."

She sat up straight and the front of her dress roundly stirred and then settled. "Con, I'm twenty-four years old. I've been promised to you since the day of my birth. If I seem brazen it's only because I feel you are so great a part of my life. I wouldn't talk this way to anyone else."

"I should hope not."

She leaned forward, adroitly switching the subject. "That

family I told you about last time. In Denver. They're in the banking business. You could—"

"We argued about that when I was over," he said, cutting her off. "I'm a cowman. Cattle is all I know."

"But you must face facts, Con. You—"

"I know. I no longer own Jawbone." Then he added, looking away, "Thanks to your father."

"I want you to know something, Con. Since the day I learned he sold those notes he held against Jawbone, I—I hated him. I didn't weep at his funeral."

"It's not a good way to talk. He was still your father."

"Don't forget you had little use for your own father."

"We didn't understand each other is all."

Twisting herself she leaned back and put her head in his lap. She looked up, watching him for a long moment. "It was a long hot ride over here, Con. If I'm to get home before dinner I'll have to leave soon."

He swallowed in a dry throat, aware of a burgeoning warmth through his body. He bent his head and kissed her and she opened her mouth. And the sharp point of her tongue put a flame along his back. Finally he drew back and looked around. There was no movement that he could see by the headquarters buildings. And here the trees were thick and the sounds of Kentucky Creek were pleasant. A jay scolded and through the green ceiling of willow he could see the clear blue of the sky.

Nelda sat up and fussed with her hair. She squirmed and turned her head and slanted her green eyes at him. "Remember the first time you saw me? I mean really saw me? In the river. I was fifteen."

"And I was a year older and gallant in those days," he said with a tight smile. "All that changed when I came back from the war." The smile turned bitter. "And I got drunk one night and—" He grabbed at a handful of grass again.

"That day along the river we were kids." Her voice lowered. "I guess we both saw suffering in the war." She had been trapped in St. Louis during most of the conflict. "Morals, conventions just don't seem to mean very much."

"We should have waited."

"Were you faithful to me during the war, Con?"

"Were you to me?"

"You have the proof that I was. A woman has no way of telling whether a man was a virgin or not."

"You seem to have obtained a rounded education at the young ladies' academy," he snapped.

"We feel it's time women became aware of life."

"Next you'll be wanting the vote."

"It will come. In time. You'll see."

"I'll probably never live to see it."

She gave a small laugh. "As I said before, I'll have to leave soon or I won't be home in time."

"Do me a favor, Nelda," he said, frowning. "If Arch starts to— Oh, I mean if he gets in any kind of trouble. If you worry about him for any reason, let me know."

"You mean because of that herd he took north? Honey, he told the truth. It was Comanches. You ask Leacham. He was with Arch."

"Leacham is an old-time cowhand. Like Charlie Baston or Timoteo. Leacham is loyal to the patron, who happens to be Arch Linnbrook. Leacham would swear the Devil wore a halo if Arch told him to. But Leacham *didn't* go with Arch. He stayed home."

"Wonder what Leacham would say if he knew that all the way over here he was sitting next to a woman who wore nothing but a green dress."

He looked around at her. "I had a hunch about that. Someday you'll get caught in a windstorm."

"I always pray for a calm day." She grinned. "I feel positively shameless, but it was so damn hot today for much clothing—"

"You know I don't like to hear you cuss like that."

"I'm sorry. Honey, with Arch getting married maybe we could make it a double wedding."

"He marrying a Texas girl?"

"No, a girl I met in St. Louis. Coralee Whitley." She caught the lobe of his ear in her teeth. "Let me write my friends in Denver," she whispered after a moment.

But she had him now and he cut her off by pressing his mouth against hers . . .

They drove back to the house and the men in the yard tipped their hats to Nelda. And Joe Leacham said, "You two have a nice drive along the creek?"

Nelda smiled and nodded and Con gave the 88 hand a sharp glance. But if Leacham meant anything by the remark it did not show on his face. Con did not press it.

When Nelda and the 88 hands had left, Con told his men about the fight with Peale. The firing of Jud Kilhaven. Timoteo had put arnica on his slashed cheek. He was helping roll Peale's body in a tarp beside the grave the 88 men had dug.

Timoteo said, "It is the same as it was in the old years. When the Comanches come. A man dead in this yard with an arrow in his throat. And then came days of fighting and days of dying."

Con clenched his teeth. "Peale the first man dead. This time another war. More blood on the ground."

After supper, later that night, Con saddled a fresh horse and rode the ten miles to Santa Margarita. He thought of the blood-letting Timoteo had prophesied. He thought of Nelda. Would marriage make it any different? Or was that all there was to it? Just the breathless thrashing about. In a house, with marriage. Not on the creek bank with the Texas sun burning into your back.

He wondered who had changed the most through the years. Himself or Nelda.

He thought of their first meeting after the war. It was at 88 and the hands were gone to town with Arch. And there was good New Orleans whisky Bert Linnbrook had not lived to drink. Oblivion and the awakening with the morning sun on Nelda's fresh and smiling face beside his own.

Chapter Four

AS HE RODE toward the town's lamp glow ahead Con thought of how the Linnbrooks had given him so much . . . and at the same time had taken so much from him. So much given to him by Mrs. Linnbrook, the giving of his very existence. So much given by her daughter, Nelda. He wondered then as he felt his after-roundup tiredness, if in time love turned from that giddy, empty feeling into something practical. Like an obligation, to a certain extent. And he was obligated to Nelda. No denying that. And under the circumstances she should be willing to wait a year until he had both of his feet planted solidly on the Texas earth once again.

And had it not been for what her father, Bert Linnbrook, had taken from him, he and Nelda would now be married. Bert Linnbrook had taken Jawbone by selling him out. On the one hand, the giving by the Linnbrooks. On the other, the taking.

He wondered if his father, lying in his worn butternut uniform somewhere in the Georgia hills with Big Ed, had turned in his grave when Bert Linnbrook's action caused Jawbone to fall into Yankee hands.

His father, Rand Jason, who had sworn to God that no man but a Jason would ever own Jawbone. He had also sworn he would live his life as he saw fit and no bearded country lawyer in a stovepipe hat was going to tell him he couldn't secede from the Union if he felt like it. And so great was his fervor that Rand Jason, after losing one command in the war, returned home to outfit a detachment of cavalry with his own money because the faltering CSA government could no longer do it for him. Borrowing heavily from his best friend and neighbor, Bert Linnbrook; never really expecting to be pressured into repayment until conditions improved.

But despite the ties between the two families, Con remembered bitterly, Bert Linnbrook sold him out shortly after the end of hostilities. Even after Con had worked hard and promised to try and repay the money his dedicated Rebel father had borrowed. But Texas wealth lay in cattle and who wanted to buy? Only later did the northern market become a reality instead of a tenuous hope.

At the livery, the night hostler, Harvey Pearce, put out a hand for the reins of Con's horse. "How's that Yankee cow outfit you're running these days, Con?" Pearce wheezed in his fat man's voice.

Con flushed. He could never come to town but what somebody didn't remind him that Jawbone was owned by Northerners.

"Things are going about as well as can be expected," he said shortly.

"You sure send a lot of mail," Pearce went on, chewing a piece of straw. He led Con's horse along the runway. "Seems like all you do for them Yankee bosses is push a pen. No time for settin' a saddle, huh?"

He turned Pearce's jibe aside. There was no denying that he was almighty sick of the whole thing. If it weren't for the plans for Nelda and himself— He was weary of the reports, from payroll to calf crop, to the sheet of tin you bought to patch the bunkhouse roof.

"Seen Charlie Baston in town?" Con asked.

"He's drunk an' sick. Got a hole in his shoulder. He's over behind Slager's."

Con swore. "He's supposed to be at Doc Maxfield's."

"What happened out at Jawbone today?"

Con didn't answer. He strode on his long legs down the darkened street, past Slager's Saloon with its horses at the tie rack. He cut through the alley beside the saloon, tramped along a path through a cottonwood grove and came to a low adobe building. He jerked open a heavy oaken door and stepped into a small room with a sofa and two tables and chairs. An empty beer bottle was on one of the tables.

A fat woman with red hair came storming along a hallway. "Nobody but a gentleman comes in here. And a gentleman always knocks on a lady's door— Oh, hello, Jason. First time I ever saw you in my establishment. I'm honored—"

"Charlie Baston's here."

"With Maude."

"Missus Oakum, do you want me to get him? Or will you do it?"

"Well, he isn't in a very presentable—"

"I'll give you two minutes."

"All right. I don't want no trouble with Jawbone. I like their Yankee money too much." Grinning, she hurried down the hallway.

Charlie Baston had time to spare before the two-minute deadline was up. He still wore the crude bandage at his shoulder. There was fever in his eyes and he looked sick, like a man who had gorged himself on spoiled meat.

"You got troubles, son?" Charlie Baston said thickly.
He smelled of Texas whisky.

"You're the one with troubles. I told you to go to Doc
Maxfield's. Instead, I find you here."

Charlie Baston scowled, fingered his rope of a mustache.
"I figured you was havin' hell in a basket out at Jawbone
an' you needed ol' Charlie to bust a few caps for you.
But if there ain't no trouble, you don't need me. Here I got
whisky to drink and a woman. You go on. son, an' leave me
alone."

"You'll see Doc," Con said firmly.

"Goddam you, Con. I washed your face for you when
you wasn't big enough to spit over the toe of your boot."

"You walking to Doc's? Or am I going to carry you?"

Charlie Baston glared, muttered into his down-curving
mustache. Then the steam seemed to run out of him. "My
arm does hurt like hell. Reckon I ain't drunk enough. Whisky
cures everything."

Con walked him out into the darkness, turned him in
the direction of Doc Maxfield's cottage. The glowing windows
could be seen through the trees. Baston staggered off, muttering to himself. Con waited until he saw the doctor's door
open and saw Baston in the shaft of lamplight. Baston went
inside. The door closed on darkness.

Con entered Slager's by the rear door. There were a
dozen or so men drinking, playing cards in the long, low-
ceilinged place. Some of them nodded. Others looked away.
Con tramped over the dirt floor to the bar. Barney Slager,
a brush of pale wiry hair topping a square face, set out a
bottle and glass. "You trailing nawth this year, Con?"

"The partners have decided to let the beef market pick up."

"That's the trouble with Yankees," Slager observed, his
voice rumbling in a thick throat. "They don't know the cow
business. They can't fight a war."

"Nevertheless, they whipped us."

Sid Millot, former sergeant with Stuart, who now ranched
over on Castle Creek, said, "They never whipped us. They
starved us out. But then I reckon it don't make no mind
to you. Seein' as how you cozy up to 'em now."

There was an uncomfortable silence and Con looked
around at the tough-featured little ex-sergeant of the CSA.

"It was that good neighbor of mine and yours—that prime *Tejano*, Bert Linnbrook, who made it possible for Yankees to own Jawbone," Con said thinly. "Alliance Cattle Company, it seems, had more faith in Texas cattle than we had."

Millot twisted his lips. "You cozying up to the same Yankees that killed your pa an' your brother, Big Ed."

Con turned his back on Millot and drank off his whisky. Millot was a bitter man for more reasons than losing a war. Millot had been one of those shirt-tail ranchers who had anted up a hundred head of cows each to make up the pool herd Arch Linnbrook had taken north last year and lost. To Comanches, Arch said.

He was remembering the day Millot stopped by on his way home from the war. "Your poppa an' Big Ed. I seen em, Con. They rode up to them Yank cannon, waving their sabers as if they figured to cut iron with 'em. There was grapeshot big as a man's thumb whipping around like bees. Your poppa and Ed and them boys riding with 'em— Well, they was so chewed up you could hardly tell hoss from man. The dirty blue-bellies could've met 'em with sabers instead of grapeshot."

"In the war you used the first weapon at hand. I know. Thank God it's over. It was good of you to stop by, Millot."

Now Con poured himself another drink and got the conversation away from the war. At least temporarily. He asked if there was any news about the deputy sheriff they had requested be stationed at Santa Margarita. They'd been trying to get a representative of the law here for six months.

"Sheriff Keeler's so busy lickin' Yankee bootstraps over San Pablo way," Slager said, "he can't worry about Texans down here."

Con said, "Barney, I may need some extra men. Pass the word around."

"You worked roundup short-handed. How come you need more men now that it's over?"

It was on the tip of Con's tongue to hint about the rustling Arch had talked of. But he decided against it. There was enough bad feeling against Arch as it was, because of that herd that was lost in Missouri. He owed Arch something, he reasoned. But Arch himself— Con felt that this was a new Arch. Not the Arch he had known before the war. Or had

Arch always been this way? Maybe that was it. He thought
of some of the things Arch and Big Ed had done. Even
though there had been five years' difference in their ages,
Arch and Big Ed had hit it off. Con had seldom gone
anywhere with his brother.

"Always good to know where you can hire on men quick,
if you need them," Con said.

"A man would have to be damn hungry to take Jawbone
money these days," Slager said heavily.

Con looked the saloonman in the eye. He reminded Slager
of the visit to Santa Margarita last year of Leroy Marcom,
one of the Alliance partners. "I don't recall you shuddering
too much, Barney," Con said, "when Marcom paid for his
whisky and his gambling with good hard Yankee dollars."

The silence stretched thin and then Mark Dollop, clerk
from the Monument Hotel across the street, threw down
his cards at a gaming table and limped up to the bar. "Don't
forget that Con fought on our side," Dollop said to Slager.
He was Slager's brother-in-law. The men had married sisters,
but both wives had since died. As Slager glared at him,
Dollop said, his thin pale face smiling wistfully, "My luck
is sour at cards tonight as usual. I wonder, Barney, could
you—"

"You know the rules I set down for you!" Slager snapped.
"I got you a job at the hotel. I give you free whisky. But
I won't fork out money for you to gamble with."

"All right, Barney," Dollop said in his mild voice. "Don't
get excited about it." He looked up at Con. "Wish I had
your two good legs. I'd try ranching myself. And get away
from that hotel desk. It's a graveyard for an active man.
But unfortunately my old saber wound—"

Con threw a coin on the bar, hoping to cut Dollop off
before the man recounted his defense of a certain sector
during the battle of Fredericksburg. "Have a drink, Mark."

"Gladly."

A man shuffled up from the shadows and turned haunted
eyes on Con. He did not look old, yet his hair was white.
He was heavy about the jowls and he had the fleshy neck of an
aging woman. "Con, I was wonderin' if you'd like to drink
to the glory of the Rebellion."

Con nodded to Slager and another glass was set out. The

man grabbed eagerly for the glass and drank off his whisky while the men watched. A few of them were smiling into the lamplight. A man laughed.

Con looked around, his eyes hard. The laughter stopped. He pushed the bottle down to the white-haired man. "Drink up, Ad," Con said.

Ad Semple nodded gratefully. He spilled whisky as he poured another drink, his hand was shaking so. Before the war he had run with Big Ed and Arch. Now he hung around Slager's, and if strangers arrived and were so inclined, Semple would show them "what dirty greasers done to a white man," in exchange for a bottle of whisky.

Mark Dollop had edged away from Semple as if the man might be victim of some dread disease. Dollop had been carrying a battered gray campaign hat under his arm. Now he set it on his rather thin hair. "The boys here, Con," Dollop said, looking around the big room, "shouldn't ride you with sharp spurs about the war. Those new men at Jawbone are former CSA."

"Yeah," Slager conceded, looking at Con. "But I can't figure 'em takin' Yankee money. I hear Kilhaven used to be with Quantrill."

Con stiffened. This was something he didn't know. "Quantrill was a butcher," he said coldly.

"He fought on our side," Dollop reminded.

"I daresay Jeff Davis took no pride in it." Con looked around. "For your information Kilhaven is fired. I had to kill his friend Peale."

Nobody said anything. Con walked to the door and Ad Semple said drunkenly, "To the glory of the Rebellion." He spilled a glass of whisky down the front of his shirt.

Chapter Five

ON THE HARD seat of the jolting coach Coralee Whitley pressed the handkerchief to her lips. Her eyes were tightly closed. There were only two passengers left, herself and the tall dark man in the good broadcloth, Bentley Hake. The other

passengers had disembarked at San Pablo. They would be in
Santa Margarita within the hour. It was dark and the coach
sidelamps cut a yellow swath into the Texas darkness. She
was glad of the comforting night. Never in her twenty years
had she seen such an awesome sight as she had witnessed
just before noon.

Bentley Hake, noticing her paleness, said, "Aren't you
over it yet?"

"I'll never be over it," she said through her teeth.

"A man hanging isn't pleasant, I admit, but—"

She closed her ears to his voice. It was cultured and once
she had found him charming. But the voice grated on her.
She had listened to it all the way from St. Louis. She was
completely disillusioned by so many things. By this man
Hake, who two nights ago had consumed more brandy than
usual and suggested they enjoy a mutual sharing in a room
at the way station where they had stopped. Disillusioned also
by the things Hake had said about Arch Linnbrook. Because
the brandy had turned Hake ugly when he couldn't get
things his own way.

"You'll have to get used to a new life in Texas," Hake
had said, no longer the charming gentleman who had known
her father. "Things aren't the same as they were in St. Louis.
New standards here. Among other things you'll have hardship
for a time. You and Arch will be on the trail for a long
time until we reach Chihuahua City."

"Arch said we would live in Texas."

"Plans have been changed. We're taking a herd to Mexico.
Several herds, in fact." Hake laughed and took a drink from
the brandy bottle. They had been standing in the dark beside
a wall of the way station.

"You're stealing cattle?" she had demanded. "Is that what
you and Arch are up to?"

"As I said, you'll have to get used to new standards here."
His hand was on her arm, her face close. "It's been a long
hard trip. Come inside. Arch will never know."

She broke away from him but he caught her by a wrist,
jerking her around so that a plait of her pale hair came
unpinned and whipped across her face. Her blue eyes were
frightened, but she put scorn in her voice. "If I told Arch,
he'd—"

Hake's fingers tightened on her wrist. She thought of screaming. But would it do any good in this rough place? Hake said, "Don't tell me you're so virtuous. St. Louis in the war with all the troops—"

"You're disgusting!"

"Birds of a feather, you know. How about your friend Nelda Linnbrook?"

"Nelda was *married* to that officer."

"So she claims, But he's dead and who's to say differently?"

"It's Nelda's life. And it's her secret. She wants it kept that way. A secret."

"Attractive widows have a certain charm."

And when Hake lifted a hand to smooth his dark hair, Coralee managed to get away from him. Lifting her hems, she rushed to her room and barred the door. The idea of returning to St. Louis was strong in her, but she had nothing there. And aside from a hundred and fifty dollars, the only money she had was the two hundred Arch had sent her.

The next morning Hake said, "Forget anything I said last night. I was a little drunk. Sorry." He gave her his white-toothed smile. But she was untouched by it.

And now in the rocking stage with the dust and the stench of old cigars and sweat, the pound of hoofs, the liberal cursing of the driver above, she made up her mind. Or, rather, seeing the man hanging today had done it for her. The brutality had brought out the core of fear in her. The man had been hanging for days. And his face was gone. Vultures, Hake had said. If this sort of thing could go on in Texas she wanted nothing to do with the place.

The stage rolled into Santa Margarita and hardly had it halted in front of a hotel than she had fumbled the coach door open, and with skirts lifted, was hurrying up the veranda steps. Hake said something to her, but she didn't turn back to see what he wanted.

In the deserted lobby she looked around at horsehair sofas and leather-bottomed chairs. There was a big iron stove in the center, cold now because of the spring heat. There was no one behind the desk, but in a few moments a thin pale man wearing a CSA campaign hat limped across the street and smiled at her.

He said his name was Mark Dollop and he was at her

service. She got a room, signed the register and took her key. She started for the stairs, Dollop bringing up her valise. She looked around. "When is the next stage west?"

"Westbound maybe in two days, ma'am. You're Arch Linnbrook's intended. He's shown your picture around." He smiled. "You and Arch honeymooning on the westbound?"

She swallowed and asked Dollop if he could furnish pen and ink and paper. He said he surely could and she wrote a note, shielding the paper from his eyes:

> Dear Arch: I am returning your
> money. Please believe me, it is
> better I find there is no love in
> my heart for you before I marry
> you.
>   Your friend, Coralee

From her reticule she took two hundred dollars put it with the note in an envelope and addressed it to *Archer Linnbrook, 88 ranch, Santa Margarita, Texas.* "Will you put this in your safe?" she said, her voice shaking.

Dollop nodded. There was puzzlement on his rather weak face, she thought, but she was thankful he asked no questions. "After I am on the westbound stage," she said, trying to sound calm, "will you see that Mr. Linnbrook gets the envelope?"

For a long moment Bentley Hake stood on the walk in front of the hotel, smoking a cheroot. The stage went on down the street, pulled in at the wagon yard. Some men had come out of the saloon across the street to witness the arrival of the stage. But they had gone back inside, the swinging doors cutting into the shards of lamplight.

He glanced at the hotel and could see Coralee at the desk. He wondered how much he had talked the other night? Well, no matter. If she told Arch, so what? He didn't care much about Arch being in the deal anyway. Arch had the temper of a wild horse. And in this game you had to have a steady hand. It was the green-eyed Nelda who had made the game interesting enough to include her brother. He had known them both in St. Louis at the tag end of the war.

Tensely he stared around at the shadows. He had no idea of just what he'd find here in Santa Margarita. He wasn't due to arrive until next month. But he had swung through St. Louis as he had promised Arch earlier, and picked up Arch's intended, Coralee. Hake had thought her company might make the trip less monotonous. But it hadn't turned out that way.

He pushed thoughts of Coralee from his mind. There were more important things at hand. They'd have to move swiftly before Alliance Cattle Company found the seven-thousand-dollar shortage in their books. A tip on a boatload of cotton carried on a Great Lakes steamer had prompted Hake to "borrow" from his other partners. The steamer sank. As a result Hake's long-range plan for stripping Jawbone of cattle suddenly became immediate.

Only one of his partners gave him any concern. It was Leroy Marcom, former major in the Union forces. And Marcom's ex-sergeant, the shotgun-carrying Al Smoot. Marcom didn't know a cow from a jackass but the man had guts, Hake had to admit.

He was sweating a little when he crossed the street and entered Slager's Saloon. The men there looked around, speculating. Hake managed a smile, brushed dust from his expensive broadcloth. His black eyes dancing, he called for a drink from a thick-chested man with pale wire brush for hair.

Glass in hand, Hake looked around. "How far is it to Jawbone? I'm one of the partners."

There was a stony silence.

Hake laughed pleasantly. "Guess I should explain. I'm the only non-Yankee partner in the company. Bentley Hake, formerly with the First Virginia Volunteers."

There was a stir of excitement when Hake offered a drink for the house. A white-haired man with strangely haunted eyes cried, "To the glory of the Rebellion."

And in a moment the man came up to Hake and whispered, "For a bottle of whisky I'll show you what them bastard greasers done to a white man."

"Some other time," Hake said, for he had caught sight of a face at the rear window of the saloon. He finished his whisky, smiled at the man behind the bar. "A jolting stage-coach is hard on a man's bladder."

He walked out the back door and into the shadowed alley. "Jud," he called.

"Over here," Jud Kilhaven said. And when Hake came up beside a shed where the shadows were deep, Kilhaven added, "When I looked in that window and seen you I almost dropped. You ain't due for a month yet."

"Slight change of plans," Hake said dryly. "You've taken care of certain matters?"

"Arch Linnbrook's a goddam fool. He keeps talkin' to Jason. But Con Jason ain't goin' to throw in with us. I told Arch from the first."

"I told you what to do in case of that eventuality."

"We tried it. Today. Jason killed Peale. Fired me."

"Peale dead." Hake whistled softly and shoved his dusty hat on the back of his head. "I planned to use his certain talents with the documents we'll need in Mexico."

"He won't copy anybody's signature now. Unless it's the devil's himself. Peale had a hole big enough in him to step in."

"What are you hanging around the back doors of saloons for?" Hake demanded quietly. "Why aren't you after Jason?"

"I'm after him. Don't worry. He was in Slager's once tonight. When he comes back I'll settle for Peale."

"Where is Jason now?"

"Down at the Doc's. I put a hole in Charlie Baston. Jason's down to see him."

Hake rubbed his jaw. God, he was tired. It had been a long fast trip down from Chicago. He'd worn out some good horses. He'd put callouses on his seat from the hard benches of the stagecoaches.

"Get Jason tonight. But get him out of town. If his body isn't found for a few days, it won't hurt us any."

"Maybe he'll stay in town. Jawbone's got a room at the hotel."

"Oh, yes. I remember. In that case it looks as if you'll have to break down a hotel door." Hake put a hand on Kilhaven's arm. "How's Arch?"

"Stupid as ever."

"And his sister."

Kilhaven took a moment to answer. "Makes a man itch just lookin' at her."

"So I've noticed." Hake gave a short laugh. "Let's not be seen together until we get things under control." He started back for the saloon. Then he looked around. "Need any help with Con Jason?"

"I never missed on a job like this with Charley Quantrill. I sure as hell won't miss on this." Kilhaven stalked away in the darkness. Bentley Hake returned to the saloon.

Chapter Six

CON TALKED TO Doc Maxfield in the latter's parlor. Doc's bald head was touched by the same lamplight that washed over the shelves of books lining the room.

"Charlie's got a nasty wound, Con," the doctor said. "Looks almost as if it were made by something big as the grapeshot that took so many of our boys. Including your poppa and Big Ed."

They went out to the veranda and Con's bitter gaze swept the length of the dust-packed ruts of the road that was the only line of communication between this remote corner of the vast empire known as Texas and the rest of the world. A block away lamp glow lay softly against tethered horses, softening the harsh angles of unpainted buildings.

Doc Maxfield touched a match to his pipe bowl, his gaze in the flame of light studying the younger man. "Seems strange, when you thing about it that some of the men—or the representatives of the men—we fought so bloodily only a short time ago now own a big chunk of our state."

"You can thank Bert Linnbrook for that. If he'd waited one more year I'd have paid him back."

"Has it made any difference between you and Arch?" The doctor cleared his throat, then added, "And Nelda?"

"Nobody ever told old man Linnbrook what to do. Least of all his own children."

"Everybody thought you and Nelda would be married right after you came back from the war."

"A man has to have his roots down deep enough so the first storm won't topple him." Con looked down at the cherry-red of the pipe bowl. "At least a man does when he figures to marry a girl like Nelda."

"A woman sticks with a man, no matter what." There was a silence. "I was in Austin," Doc said, staring into the darkness, "when your father and your mother left for the Big Bend. People thought they were crazy and that they'd never last a year because the Comanches were out then. I was a young man and your brother Ed was a baby. I remember how your mother looked on the seat of that wagon. She was a pretty woman, Con. You were named for her brother. But I suppose you knew that."

"Poppa never told me."

"I'm not surprised. Your mother's people came from Kentucky. Your father never got along with them." Doc Maxfield knocked the dottle from his pipe and rested a hand on Con's arm. "I'm only saying this so you'll understand that other girls have attended fine female academies and expected more ease in life than maybe a lot do in these times. Your mother, I'm talking about."

"She must have loved the old man to come out to a wilderness like this."

"I don't suppose she wanted to come," Doc said. But it was what her husband wished. It was all the reason she needed. I'm telling you this because Nelda doesn't need to be packed in silks, insulated from life. Tell her how you want to live. If she's the right sort, and I'm sure she is, she'll do whatever you want and make a life for you both."

"Doc, I've got another year. I'm taking most of my pay in cows. I'll take up land in the Chisos—"

"Don't wait. You have no idea how very short life really is. I came here a month after you were born. I was a young man then. Now so many have gone—" His voice trailed off and he said, "Your father, for instance. He died in bitterness."

"Charging cannon with saber."

"Suicide, Con. I'll always believe that. If he couldn't live in the world he wanted he didn't want to live at all."

"Sometimes I wonder if I hated him."

"You had reasons enough," Doc Maxfield said gravely. "But it's not a thing for a man to say about his father."

"I think it started the day he burned my books."

"You made the mistake of getting your books from an Abolitionist. Your father had strong ideas on the slave question."

"But then you loaned me your own books." Con touched the doctor's shoulder. "That's the best education I ever had."

"You pass on what you can to the next generation. It's about the only valid reason for existence."

Con felt a stirring of old memories, of half-formed images. He looked down at the stocky figure of this man he had known for so long. "Tell me, Doc," he said gently, "a little more about those days in Austin."

Doc Maxfield dropped the hot pipe into his coat pocket. "There's not much to tell. Just that day when your family left for the Big Bend here. There was Timoteo, also young then. Handsome, and with a guitar slung from his saddle horn. And Charlie Baston, a hellion if there ever was one."

"But a loyal hellion."

"I tell you, Con, I'd have bet my best pair of boots against a penny whistle that Charlie would be hanged before he reached twenty-five. And now he's lying in yonder and I may not be able to save his arm. Or even his life if he doesn't behave."

Con swallowed. "I mean tell me the rest of it in Austin. You coming all the way out here. A man with talent, wasting it in a place like this."

"Just coincidence."

Con shook his head. "Once the old man broke his arm. But he wouldn't ride in and let you set it. Timoteo did it for him. And it was a bad job. The old man said he'd take an ax and cut off the arm before he'd let you set it." .

"At times your father was mule-headed."

"I never realized how much he hated you, Doc. Until that day. It's a wonder he didn't try to drive you out."

"A doctor in a frontier settlement such as this," Maxfield said dryly, "enjoys a certain immunity."

"You knew my mother back in Austin."

"In Kentucky." The doctor sighed deeply. "By the time I made up my mind not to wait any longer she had gone to

Austin to visit an aunt. There she met your father. He cut quite a dashing figure in those days. They ranched around Austin for a spell, then came out here."

"And then you came out here."

"I was curious as to what had happened to her. I intended to make my inquiries and leave. But she died a month before I arrived. I—I never forgave your father for not being with her—" Doc Maxfield gave a violent shake of his head. "Never mind, it's all in the past now."

"You don't have to spare the old man," Con said, his voice hardening. "I know what he was doing the night I was born. He told me. He was drunk along the river with a wench—"

"If you've learned one thing tonight, it's the awesome fact that the sands in a man's hourglass spill out with terrible swiftness. The older he gets the faster they fall. Marry Nelda, if she's your choice. Don't wait."

Con walked down the steps, then looked back. "Do the best you can for Charlie Baston."

As he moved along the rutted street he thought of the things this day had brought. The unreeling of the past. He angled for the Monument Hotel, thinking of the room upstairs that Jawbone paid for by the year. The Alliance Cattle Company wouldn't give him more men, he thought bitterly, but they'd throw away money on a hotel room just in case one of the partners came to Santa Margarita and didn't care to "rough it" at the ranch.

He felt that he could sleep for a week. As he entered the lobby a tall girl wearing a black dress came out of the hotel dining room. Behind her were two cattlemen, picking their teeth. They nodded to Con and went outside.

The girl's blue eyes swept over Con. And from behind his desk Mark Dollop said, "Con, this is Coralee Whitley. From St. Louis. Arch Linnbrook's intended."

As Con removed his hat, he saw the look of pain Arch's name seemed to bring the girl. But she did manage to give him a smile with her very white teeth. There was strength more than dazzling beauty in her face. Her nose was good and her mouth firm, yet he had the feeling that under certain conditions it could be relaxed enough to stir a deep fire in a man.

She claimed her key and Mark Dollop said, "I was just telling her, Con, that our accommodations here aren't the best. But even so, its luxury compared to the camps we had in the war. Like at Fredericksburg, Con. I could give you some stories—"

Coralee Whitley said, "Will you excuse me, gentlemen." And looking around at Con, her very blue eyes seemed to weight him. Then she moved toward the stairway, lifting the hems of a black dress cut for style, not for mourning. The wash of light from a bracket lamp brought out the deep yellow of her hair.

Thoughtfully he put on his hat, wondering how a rough unprincipled man like Arch Linnbrook could claim a girl like this.

Then he was aware that Dollop was saying, "She came in on the stage with one of the Alliance men. Bentley Hake."

Con wheeled, staring at Barney Slager's brother-in-law. "Hake!"

"He's at Slager's." Dollop came around the end of the desk. "I was wondering, Con, that as one former CSA man to another, if you'd stake me to a game tonight. I feel my luck is definitely on the rise and—"

Con hurried out into the darkness.

In Slager's he noted the sudden silence. He saw the tall dark man with the dancing eyes. The man wore a black suit and his shirt was wrinkled. His hat was on the back of his head. He was smiling at Con and Barney Slager, meaty hands on his bartop, was saying, "Here he is now, Mr. Hake."

With every eye on him Con moved up to the bar. Hake put out his hand. His clasp was strong. So this was the man whose signature he had seen so many times on letters from Alliance. "Welcome to Texas," Con said.

"It's a pleasure. You met Leroy Marcom last year."

"I had the pleasure of the major's company, yes."

Slager grinned. "This ain't no Yankee, Con. He was on our side."

"With Quantrill, by any chance?"

Hake's dark eyes turned cold. He straightened and Con could see the heelplates of a revolver under his coat. "Sir, that could be construed as an insult in some quarters."

Con was aware of the stiffening silence. He shrugged. "You forced two of your friends on me. I heard that one of them was with Charley Quantrill."

"You must be referring to Kilhaven and Peale," Hake said thinly. "They're employees, not friends. If one of them was with Quantrill, I didn't know it."

Con glanced around at the faces in the long, shadowed room with its bar and polished glass and oiled dirt floor and gaming tables. "Barney, did you tell him about Kilhaven and Peale?"

"No," Slager said.

Hake's black brows lifted in inquiry and Con thought, He'd be a charmer to a woman. A woman like that Coralee Whitley?

He told Hake how he had been forced to kill Peale and fire Kilhaven.

"Don't let that bother you," Hake said with a cutting gesture. "That pair were highly recommended. If they gave you trouble, it's better to be rid of them. A drink, Lieutenant?"

Con nodded and with a glass in his hands, he said, "Your Yankee partners hold no ill-feeling because you were their enemy?"

"When there is profit involved," Hake said, lifting his glass, "a man forgets his memories of the war."

Con looked around. "I wish people down here could forget the war."

"I may take money from Yankees," Hake said, his eyes glittering, "but I hate their bleeding guts!"

A Rebel yell swept Slager's and Hake smiled at the men and then let his amused gaze come to rest on Con. Con said, "Nelda Linnbrook is a friend of a Miss Whitley of St. Louis. And you brought Miss Whitley to Santa Margarita. So I'm assuming you know Arch."

"He served under me for a time. I look forward to seeing Arch again."

"Like most Texans," Con said, looking him in the eye, "Arch is a little beaten down these days. He used to have forty men and now he had eight at the last count. And his cow count is also down. But Arch has grand plans for the future."

"I daresay," Hake said. He smothered a yawn, muttering that he'd had a long ride on the coach and was dead for sleep. "You'll be riding to Jawbone tonight, Jason?"

"It's ten miles and the hour is getting late."

"Then we'll stay at the hotel. You take the Jawbone room and I'll get one of my own."

Con watched the broad black-clad back move across the barroom, a slim brown hand lifting to the men. The men said, "G' night, Captain." And when Hake had gone, somebody said, "I feel a heap different about Alliance Cattle Company now."

Slager said, "Hake oughta kick his Yankee partners out and take Jawbone for himself. How about that, Con?"

"He's probably given it some consideration."

Billy Snider, a wiry man whose side whiskers looked white as snow-laden brush in the Chisos, said, "What sort of plans has that thievin' Arch Linnbrook got now?"

Con looked around. Snider was neighbor to ex-sergeant Millot. Con said, "You'll know Arch's plans in time."

"Maybe he's got plans to take some more cows nawth!" Billy Snider's voice cracked. "But he won't get mine again. The son of a bitch!"

"You can't blame Arch for what Comanches done to that herd," Barney Slager said in defense.

Snider made a sound with his lips like the breaking of wind from a large horse.

Ad Semple's haunted eyes were on Con. "A toast to your poppa and Big Ed and the Glory of the Rebellion——"

"Oh, kee-ryst, Ad," Barney Slager said, "you've had enough toastin' the Rebellion for one night."

"What else has he got to live for but whisky?" a man snickered.

Con went out, stood looking at the hotel across the street. He thought of the pale-haired girl in the black dress. A girl who had shared a coach with Bentley Hake all the way from St. Louis.

Remembering his conversation with Doc Maxfield tonight, Con suddenly made up his mind.

He rode west through the night, toward the Linnbrook 88 ranch.

He was a mile out of town when a deeper shadow in a field of shadows beside the stage road alerted him. He had been aware of the possibility of trouble and was riding with rifle loose in the boot, his revolver hiked around for easy reaching. Drawing his rifle, he swung down all in one easy movement. His horse ran on a few yards and nickered.

There was an answering whinny and a man's harsh voice said, "Goddam that hoss—"

A winking eye briefly put a hole in that night and a bullet slammed past Con's face. He felt its whistling breath against his cheek. He fired at the flash and heard a horse go pounding off. Another shot from the ambusher's rifle screamed off at the moon.

Aiming at the powder flash, Con let go. He emptied the rifle just for luck. But he could hear the horse in the distance now and knew he had likely missed his target.

Sweating, he listened. The hoofbeats were only a bare sound now above the whisper of the night wind through the huisache that dotted the basin.

He rode on, extra careful now. Miles later he saw the buildings of 88 ahead. Even though it was nearly midnight, there was a glow of light at the house windows.

He rode down into the yard and thought of the times he had come here as a boy. The shortness of life, Doc Maxfield had stressed tonight. He remembered the slashing bullet out there in the darkness. Jud Kilhaven's voice cursing his noisy horse. He was sure of that much.

There was a film of cold sweat on his brow when he swung down in the Linnbrook yard.

Chapter Seven

EVEN THOUGH THE hour was late Arch Linnbrook met Con in the yard. Arch was a little drunk. He seemed strangely silent when Con told him about Charlie Baston being shot. How Jud Kilhaven had tried for an ambush outside town tonight.

Arch said, after Con had unsaddled and they were walking

to the house, "The spare room's made up. Nelda will be glad for you to stay over."

"I'll have to leave in the morning."

"Nelda will be some disappointed."

"I want to have a talk with her before I go." Con hesitated. The moon made yellow ironwork of cottonwood branches. "I've changed my mind about some things, Arch."

Arch halted. "Then you're comin' in with us. Nelda—"

"So Nelda knows about it," Con said, his voice tight. "And she approves."

"I didn't want to tell her. But she kept after me. She said you hinted around about somethin'." Arch looked around. They were on the porch. "What did you figure to talk to her about? If it wasn't that?"

"I was going to tell her I want to marry her. And do a little pioneering. As our own folks did in the old days." He clenched his hands. "Maybe it's too much to ask."

In the parlor with its brown-framed portraits of the late Bert Linnbrook and his wife, Arch filled glasses. Against the wall were sofas, polished brass at the stone hearth. The windows were curtained with the lace that Nelda sent all the way to Paso to be laundered.

"Con, I'm askin' you one more time," Arch said, handing him a glass. "Come in with me. We're friends. I'm closer to you than if you was my brother. And I always had the feelin' you was closer to me than you ever was to Big Ed."

"Arch, I can't—" Con's gaze settled on the portrait of Mrs. Linnbrook and her sad eyes seemed to be watching him. And he thought of her breast that had given life to him.

Arch drank off his whisky too fast and coughed. "If you're on my side of the fence, Con—" He broke off, staring at the last drop of amber fluid trapped at the bottom of his glass.

Con tore his gaze from the portrait of Arch's mother. "Don't go ahead with this thing, Arch!"

"It's too late!" A bright edge of the old Arch Linnbrook rage appeared in the gray eyes. "Goddam you, Con. You're as mulish as your old man was!"

"You're walking in quicksand, Arch. If you don't stop you'll be in over your head!"

"We can be rich, Con!" Arch clenched a big hand into

a fist. "Don't it mean anything that we'll be able to hold our heads up again?"

"Since when can a thief ever hold up his head?"

"Get out of here!" Arch cried, his voice shaking. "Before I kick your head to pieces."

"Don't lay a hand on me, Arch. I warned you about that. I won't fist-fight you!"

Con started backing to the door and Arch suddenly wilted. "Don't go, Con, I—"

And from behind Con, Nelda said, "You're sleeping here, Con. I made your bed myself."

Con looked around. She stood in the hall, long coppery hair loose about a pale-green wrapper, its high collar turned up around her neck. Her green eyes seemed alert, but she yawned and said, "See you for breakfast, honey." And when he hesitated, she added, "I mean it, Con. You stay here tonight." Then to her brother, "You go to bed directly, Arch. You hear? Don't you go staying up all night again with a bottle in your lap."

She blew Con a kiss. Then with a soft padding of bare feet she was gone. Outside, two cats suddenly broke the stillness with their nerve-jarring sounds of courtship.

Con said, "Arch, Coralee Whitley's in town. Bentley Hake brought her."

Arch's face turned white. "At a time like this she comes." Then he searched Con's face intently. "You saw Hake? You talked to him?"

"I did. He's your partner in this. Am I right?"

Arch turned and picked up the bottle and drank from it. Con went to the room he always used here. After he undressed down to his underwear, he lay down in the dark. For the first time in the years he had visited here, he pushed a loaded pistol under the blankets.

He waited and in a few minutes Nelda slipped quietly into the room and sat on the edge of his bed. "Arch told me about his scheme for getting rich," she said.

"I know." He could barely see her face in the darkness. "You find the idea appealing?"

She leaned down, pressed against him, and the billowing nightdress clung to her. She kissed him, and when there was no response, she said, "You're angry."

"Call it disappointment."

"Because I want money?"

"Disappointed that you want me to steal it."

She gave an angry push at the long hair shadowing one side of her face. "Can't you understand that since the war nothing is the same? Nothing will ever again be the same?"

"How does your friend Coralee feel about it?" He told her of the girl's arrival on the stage tonight.

Nelda seemed surprised. "We didn't expect her so soon. But now that she's here we can have that double wedding—"

"She came with Bentley Hake."

"Oh?" And Con felt the stiffening of her body. "I'm sure Coralee will make a good wife for Arch."

"Money is important to her?"

"Her family owned riverboats and warehouses in St. Louis. The Yankees commandeered what they didn't sink. I lived with them for a time when I couldn't get back to Texas because of the war." Nelda went on to say that losing his fortune killed Coralee's father. And her mother died soon after. "Of course money is important to her. What else is there?"

"I guess I had the fool's dream tonight. Thinking I could convince you to marry me and live down in the Chisos. Because life is so short."

"I love you very much, Con, but—"

"But not enough for that. To build a life as your mother and father built their lives."

"Do you think they were happy? My mother died young because of hardship."

"Cholera came that year. It struck down those living a life of ease. As well as those with hardships."

"Your own mother didn't die of cholera," Nelda reminded him sharply. "She died giving birth to you and because there was no doctor."

"There's a doctor here now." And when she made a squirming movement of displeasure, he said with soft intensity, "Just what is it you would have me do?"

"There's a rich Mexican who is going to buy all the beef—" She broke off, hugging him against the front of her nightdress. "Con, love me first, then we can talk."

"A rich Mexican and stolen cattle. And living like a *rico* in Chihuahua City. You want me to become a thief."

Her mouth moved warmly across his face. "I want your child, Con," she whispered. "This time I want your child."

"And so you'll try and shame me into disregarding my principles. In order to give my son a good life?"

"You're very sure it will be a boy." Her voice was hoarse. "I'll try. I'll try very hard. Nine months from tonight he'll be born in Mexico. And his parents will be very rich."

Quickly he rolled away from her and got up. He put on his clothes in the dark. She uttered not a sound but he could feel her fury.

He went into the front part of the house. Arch was asleep in the chair, snoring, an empty bottle at his feet.

When Con went down to the corral, Joe Leacham, clad in his underwear, holding rifle and lantern watched him from the bunkhouse door.

In the saddle, Con turned to the cowhand, seeing the weathered face in the lantern glow. "Joe, try and keep Arch on a tight rein."

"The rein ain't been made that's tight enough to hold him."

"I hope we don't have a war hereabouts, Joe."

"It's shapin' up," Leacham said laconically.

"You'll side with Arch, no matter what?"

"Reckon I don't know no better. Take care, Con."

"See you, Joe."

Con rode off into the night.

Chapter Eight

NELDA LAY ON the bed and beat her fists and put a corner of a blanket into her mouth so Arch couldn't hear her sobs. Not that he likely would, drunk as he was. Her tears were hot and she felt nausea and an urge to run out into the darkness and scream Con's name. But when she heard him ride out she did not stir from the bed.

Because she had wanted to get away and think about

Con, for the second time that afternoon she had ridden toward the Jawbone west line. There was a chance she might see Con. And she knew that she *had* to convince him that Arch was right. Arch's revelation had staggered her. Maybe ten thousand head of cattle to be sold in Mexico. Stripping the range of every available head of beef. Con must understand that she could no longer live in Texas. Chihuahua City was exciting. They could go to Mexico City. Or Europe for a visit. She'd raise her children in the elegant surroundings she had witnessed briefly in St. Louis before those who favored the Southern cause were finally ruined financially.

No matter what else had happened, she loved Con. He belonged to her.

Shadows were long when she reached the Jawbone line. But there was no sign of Jawbone riders. The ranch headquarters was only eight miles east. She could ride over and Con would be forced to put her up for the night. But she was afraid to ride after dark.

Turning her horse, she started for home.

And it was then she was startled by the horseman riding out of a draw. Her mouth dry, she watched him approach slowly. She fumbled for the revolver she always carried in a saddlebag. But then she recognized the man. It was Jud Kilhaven, the new *segundo* at Jawbone. And he had been over at the house several times, drinking with Arch, their heads together.

"Evenin', Miss Linnbrook," Kilhaven said, touching his hat brim.

"Is Con Jason over this way by any chance?"

"Ain't seen him, ma'am." He rode up close, gave her a lazy look with his muddy eyes. He rubbed his long jaw and looked her over in a manner she didn't like at all. She felt a sharp anger. He said, "I been fired. You know that."

She started to spur her horse, but Kilhaven grabbed it by a headstall and when the mount swung around she was nearly unseated. She reached for her revolver again, but Kilhaven only laughed. His wrists were thick. His long hair hung down on either side of his face.

"Some fond of Con Jason, ain't you, ma'am."

"That's my business. And if you don't turn loose of my horse, I'll tell him. And he'll—"

"He'll what, ma'am?"

"Kill you.'

"Reckon he'll try. He'll sure try, ma'am."

He would not release his grip on the headstall of her restless horse. A deep fear began to boil in her. His knee touched hers. He was grinning.

"When I was with ol' Charley we had some times," Kilhaven said.

"You mean Charlie Baston?" she said, trying to keep him talking so she could plan some way to get rid of him.

"Charley Quantrill, ma'am." The muddy eyes looked her over again. "We had a lot of what you call the spoils of war."

She felt heat on her face. "A pack of rapists!"

"Gets in your blood. The war's over, but them times stick with a man."

She leaned over the saddle horn, her green eyes blazing. "Turn me loose in one second or I'll tell my brother!"

Kilhaven laughed.

"He'll break you in two!"

"If he got his hands on me, sure. A bullet reaches some distance, ma'am."

There was a thrashing in the brushy draw where Kilhaven had appeared and she felt a brief hope. Kilhaven had twisted in the saddle, his gun swinging up. But it was only a Jawbone cow with calf.

And while he was turned she spurred her horse and it sprang forward with a scream of pain. Kilhaven's hold was broken. With the wind in her face she thought she had gotten away from him. But he came pounding behind, gaining. She fumbled her revolver out of the saddlebag, but dropped it.

Then he was abreast of her, his long arm about her waist. Feet kicking the air, she was drawn out of the saddle. He held her while her horse ran on ahead. Then he swung down with her. She tried to run, but he grabbed her. He flung her heavily so that when her back struck the ground the breath was jarred out of her.

"If you do this," she said in a low, deadly voice, "I'll kill you. So help me God, I'll kill you."

"I want to be friends, ma'am." His arm pinned her flat.

"Friends!" she cried, her lips trembling. "This is a friendship I don't care for."

"How was that friendship in St. Louis? The one with that Johnny Reb from Georgia. You was lonely and he had leave and you married him. Mrs. Jonathan Edgely. The Widow Edgely now, ain't it, ma'am?"

Stunned, she peered up into the muddy eyes. "How—how did you know *that!*"

"Ways of findin' things out, ma'am."

She turned her head, her heart pounding.

Kilhaven said softly, "Be a fine state if Con Jason knowed that the woman he was fixin' to marry was widowed by the war. Now wouldn't it?"

And through her mind screamed many possibilities. What would have happened had she, upon her return to Texas, told Con the truth. That in boredom— No, not boredom. In desperation, would be better. In desperation, because she thought she would never see him again, she had married Jonathan Edgely. And Con saying, "It's all right. The war wasn't easy on any of us."

But she hadn't done it that way. She had let Con get drunk. And pretend that it was all new to her. And the next morning she had described the pain to him and the making a woman of her.

And she knew now that if he learned of her trickery he would hate her.

Through her narrowed eyes she looked up at the face, shadowed now in the growing darkness.

"Don't hurt me," she said. "It's all I ask."

And when he rode back to the house with her much later, Arch and the men were just going out to look for her.

With a lantern held high, Arch glared at Kilhaven. "What're you doin' with Nelda?"

"Her hoss run off when she was a settin' out yonder." Kilhaven jerked a thumb over his shoulder. "I happened along an' caught him. Ain't that right, ma'am?"

She looked around at him, slouched in the saddle, that lazy grin touched by lantern light. And she had an unholy urge to scream the truth. And watch him kick his life away at the end of a rope. But he would blurt out the truth about the marriage even Arch didn't know about. And the men would talk and it would get back to Con.

She said, "Thank you for your courtesy, Mr. Kilhaven."

"Just call me Jud, ma'am. I'll be comin' over regular. To talk about the old days in St. Louis."

But when she was walking toward the house, she heard her brother say, "Keep away from her. She's promised to Con Jason. . . . What's this about you shootin' Charlie Baston?"

And now, lying in the darkness, with the sound of Con's horse fading in the night, she thought of the irony this day had brought. Lying rigid with Kilhaven's breath against her throat. Payment for his silence. And after the payment made, no longer reason for silence. Con hated her. He couldn't hate her any more if he learned of her virginal masquerade on that certain night.

But she would get him back. Somehow she would get him back. No matter how.

And in the darkness her tear-stained face was smiling. But the tears still flowed.

Chapter Nine

AT DAYLIGHT CON ate Sam Trench's steak and sourdough biscuits. When the meal was over he asked Timoteo to come up to the house. There he told the old Mexican about the arrival of the Alliance Cattle Company partner from Chicago.

"You have troubles, Chico," Timoteo said, fingering the gash on his cheek.

And Con nodded. He thought longingly of his own herd in Caballo Canyon. Two days ago he and Timoteo had scouted a good portion of the Jawbone range because there had been suspicious activity reported along the river. On a ledge above the five-mile Caballo Canyon, Con had looked down at his four hundred cows grazing on the lush grass. Cows in his own name. With his C brand. The C for Conrad. The C also for Carter, his mother's name. It had been

intended that it also would be the name of the first son
Nelda would give him.

But now when he thought of her he turned sour inside.
Two days before, he had still had plans for her.

He remembered Timoteo sitting in the shade of the Jawbone lineshack. "This sweetheart of yours," the Mexican
had said. "She will be happy down here?" And Timoteo
waved a slim brown hand at the peaks crowding against the
sky.

"Yes," Con had answered. "And you and Charlie will
work for us."

"*Rancho del Viejos,*" Timoteo said with a laugh. "Ranch
of the old ones. You do not have to watch out for us, Chico."

"As long as I live, you and Charlie will have jobs."

Timoteo had looked at him a long moment, then said,
"You are a good man, Chico. No matter what they say."

"And what do they say, old friend?"

For a moment Timoteo was silent, then he got up,
scratched himself. "They say you are a lover of the *Yanqui.*"

"I'm not a lover of Yankees. But I hold with the idea that
if you take a man's money, you must be loyal to that man."

Then they had ridden south, along the towering bluffs
above the river. A thousand feet below, the Rio twisted cool
and green through the dun-colored hills of Mexico. For
several minutes Con sat his saddle, peering down at a thick
grove of willows on the south shore. For years the place had
been used intermittently by rustlers from both sides of the
line. Some early settler had dubbed it Vega Verde.

Timoteo had pointed at the dots moving below. "When you
were a niño, I once ride down there with your father. That
day we hung the fruit of woman to the limbs of trees. Six
men dead that day."

"Hanging is what a rustler deserves," Con had said.

For half an hour they watched the dots below. That night
they had camped in the mountains. Timoteo, sitting with a
serape over his shoulders, sang of his youth. The fire burned
low. They talked of rustling.

"Those were tough days in Texas," Con said. "The hanging of rustlers. I'm afraid they will come again."

"Sí. Your brother was always ready with the rope."

Con had studied the firelighted face a moment. "You hated Big Ed."

"Your brother was son of the patron. You do not hate the son of the patron."

"Big Ed and Arch. They considered it sport to stalk the women of your race."

Timoteo poked at the fire and said nothing.

"And my father laughed when they did it," Con said.

"He was the patron."

"Like a hang rope for a rustler. There are ways of discouraging such things."

"You mean the *cuchillo*."

"Yes, the knife. Applied at certain areas." Con had shivered then. "It chills a man to think of it."

"My people have the blood of *indios* in their veins. They do not find it hard to cut with a knife . . . if there is deep reason for the cutting."

"I'm glad Arch and Big Ed had the fear put in them before it was too late. There hasn't been a Mexican girl raped in this part of Texas for years."

"One day Ad Semple will die," Timoteo grunted. "And the story of his cutting will die with him. Then it will start again. Until there is more cutting."

And now this morning Con said, "You asked the other day if my girl would live down in the Chisos. She won't. I have the final word on that, old friend."

Timoteo said nothing. Behind him the sun lifted the gray lid of a new day.

In the room of his birth, now used as an office, Con wrote several letters. To each of the partners of Alliance, telling them of his suspicions, concerning their other partner, Bentley Hake. He also wrote a letter to Sheriff Keeler at San Pablo. He outlined his problems here and asked that a deputy be sent to Santa Margarita immediately.

Then he gave the letters to Timoteo. He asked the Mexican to mail them in San Pablo. Just in case anyone in Santa Margarita had notions of preventing them from getting in the mail sack.

"You do this to get rid of me, Chico," Timoteo said severely. "You think I am too old to fight."

"I need your help, old friend. Do this thing."

Timoteo stared at him a moment. Then, shrugging, he put the letters under his shirt and rode out on his black horse, sitting his Chihuahua saddle.

An hour later, Jud Kilhaven, crouched in the brush that bordered the stage road a mile west of Santa Margarita, saw the Mexican approach. It was the first rider he had seen this morning. After a night in the brush he was in a foul mood. After his try at killing Con Jason last night his luck seemed bad. First off, Jason had sensed the ambush and swung down in time. Then Kilhaven's horse had been spooked by a slicing bullet from the barrage laid down by Con Jason. The horse ran a mile and suddenly piled up. Somehow in that wild ride for his life, his revolver had been jarred from its holster. And even though with the coming of daylight he had back-tracked the horse, he could not find the weapon in the thick brush. To sour his luck even further, he found that his rifle had become wedged between the dead horse and a slab of rock. The loading lever was badly bent, the trigger smashed off.

So he had sat out the night, not wishing to risk walking to town. There was a possibility Jason was there. Or some of the Jawbone men. It was bad enough he had struck down Timoteo with a gun barrel and shot Charlie Baston. And made a try for Con Jason from the ledge above the mesa. But after making another attempt on Jason's life last night, there would be no telling what might happen.

He didn't care to risk Texas wrath, which in a lawless area such as this, might take the form of a saddle rope cracking a man's neck.

It was not a comforting situation when a man was unarmed and dehorsed. And when the war for Jawbone beef had already started.

He was just about to make up his mind that all he could do was walk to town and take a chance that Hake had not yet gone to Jawbone. And then he saw Timoteo approaching.

Kilhaven lay down in the brush beside the road, and turned his back and put his hat over his face. Tensely he listened to the approach of the Mexican's black horse.

It was time his luck had a change for the better, Kilhaven

thought. Three times he'd been close to killing Con Jason. They'd have had him good if that stupid Peale hadn't frozen on him there in the lean-to doorway.

But then it hadn't been all bad at that. Nelda Linnbrook had been the only good thing so far. Lying on his side with the morning sun beating against his shirt, he had to smile when he remembered the scene last evening. It never hurt a man to have a good memory. And sometimes you could put that knowledge to good usage. Such as pressuring a woman—

Timoteo's black horse was a dozen yards down the road. Kilhaven groaned. He heard the Mexican rein in and say, "Qué es?"

But Kilhaven, face turned from the road, did not say what had happened to put him down like this. He groaned again. All he wanted was for Timoteo to get close enough. When that happened Kilhaven would rearm and once again have a good horse under him. Let the damn Mexican be the one to walk back to town with an empty holster.

The crunch-crunch of the black's hoofs drew nearer. Like a suddenly released spring, Kilhaven surged up from the ground. The fingers of his right hand snagged the black's headstall.

Startled, Timoteo jerked back the reins. The black reared, snorting. Kilhaven was hauled intto the air. He lost his hat and his long hair came down over his eyes. But he hung onto the headstall and made a blind stab with his left hand toward the Mexican's belt. His fingers hooked leather, jarring loose the gun Timoteo had tried to draw. Kilhaven dragged the Mexican down with him. As they struck the ground the black veered away.

Half-stunned from the fall, Timoteo tried to roll aside. The gashed cheek had started to bleed again. With an oath, Kilhaven got him by the front of the shirt, tearing it open. Some letters spilled out.

And in that moment when Kilhaven saw the Alliance Cattle Company address on one of the letters, Timoteo squirmed away. But Kilhaven snatched up the revolver the Mexican had dropped. He turned, leveling it, "Hold it, old man," but Timoteo was dragging out a pistol from under the torn shirt.

Sound smashed from Kilhaven's hand as the gun hammer

snapped down. Timoteo fell over on his side. His forehead was centered by a small blue hole.

Tensely Kilhaven looked around. There was nobody on the road. And there seemed to be no undue activity in the direction of the town. For a moment he stood there, but no one appeared. Then, holstering the revolver, he went after the black horse that had become tangled up in the brush.

Using the Mexican's saddle rope, he dragged the body some distance from the road. Still no one had ridden out from town to investigate the gunshot. Not that Kilhaven really expected this. But you could never tell. A gunshot was about as common in this corner of Texas as steak for breakfast.

When he got back to the road he was startled to see a man weaving along the ruts from town. Alarm swept through Kilhaven. And then he recognized that loco old drunk, Ad Semple. Semple staggered off the road and Kilhaven remembered then that he'd heard the man lived in a shack somewhere out in the brush.

While Kilhaven tried to make up his mind whether to go after the man or forget it, he saw a freight outfit pull out of town. Heading in his direction. That settled it. Kilhaven set spurs to the black and got away before those on the freighter could get near enough to identify him.

Kilhaven rode to 88, and when Arch Linnbrook saw the horse he was riding, he demanded to know what had happened. Kilhaven wasted no words telling him.

Arch went white. "You've done it now," he breathed. "Con won't ever rest till he's got you dead."

"He'll be the one dead."

"But I don't want that. Damn it, that's why I wanted him to come in with us peaceful. Now you've—"

"Hold on a minute," Kilhaven said coldly. "The Mex had a hideout. There was nothin' else for me to do but kill him."

Arch's eyes, bloodshot from last night's whisky, suddenly narrowed. Without warning he hit Kilhaven in the face, knocking him unconscious.

Kilhaven still lay in the yard when Bentley Hake rode in from town on a livery stable horse. He listened to the story of Timoteo's death. "Well, it can't be helped. We have more important things to worry about."

With some whisky, Hake brought Kilhaven around. The lank ex-Quantrill man got slowly to his feet. There was a swelling under his right eye. He looked at Arch for a long moment.

Hake said, "I want no grudges, understand? That goes for the two of you."

Kilhaven just stood there and finally he picked up his hat and beat the dust out of it. "No grudge," he said thinly.

Arch said, "I was just fixin' to go to town an' see Coralee."

"That will have to wait," Hake snapped. He was scanning the letters Kilhaven had taken from Timoteo. "Arch, you can see now that we have to move fast. How about it, Jud? Any Jawbone cows bunched that we can start with?"

"A thousand head on a mesa," Jud Kilhaven said, his narrowed gaze still on Arch.

"Good," Hake said. "We'll ride down to Vega Verde and get the boys—" At that moment Nelda came to the porch, wearing a green silk dress. Hake removed his hat.

She said, "Can I see you a minute, Bentley?"

"Sure." Hake looked at Arch. "You and Jud take your men down to the river. I'll catch up."

When they had ridden out, Nelda said, "Bentley, I overheard something I think you should know."

"You look pretty serious. What is it?"

"Jud Kilhaven plans to shoot you in the back and take the cattle for himself."

"Where did you hear this?"

"Never mind. I just heard it."

"So this is the sort of welcome I get in Texas," Hake said.

"If I were you, I'd kill him the first chance I got."

"I see what you mean." Hake stared at the dust of the departing men. "Maybe you'd better give me all the details, Nelda."

"Come inside," she said.

Chapter Ten

WHEN BENTLEY HAKE made no appearance at Jawbone during the day, Con decided to go into Santa Margarita and check on the man. At noon he had sent most of his men out to scout the range. If they noted any unusual activity, they were to report back to headquarters.

Con arrived in town shortly after the supper hour, with lamp glow softening the false fronts of the buildings along Houston Street. A sharp anger touched him when he walked into Slager's and saw Charlie Baston, hooting drunk, playing poker with Mark Dollop. The hotel clerk was as fired with Texas coal as was Baston.

If Baston's bad shoulder pained him any he gave no sign. Con walked over. One of the men said Baston had been playing for an hour. Billy Snider, white side whiskers damp from sweat, was shuffling the cards for Baston.

Con said, "Charlie, you should be in bed. At Doc Maxfield's."

Baston took a drink out of his bottle, tipped a little in his chair, then righted himself. "Nobody keeps me in bed! As long as I can get an honest shuffle from Billy here." With his good hand he slapped Snider on a bony arm.

Baston laboriously dealt the cards with one hand. Dollop, sitting rigid across the table, licked his lips. His eyes looked sick. Charlie Baston had most of the chips.

"Charlie," Con said thinly, "you won't be much help to me with only one arm. Now quit this foolishness and get back to Doc's."

"Dollop here," Baston said, nodding at his opponent, "took fourteen dollars from me after last roundup. By God, I'm gettin' it back. And more."

"Poker's no medicine for a sick man. Whisky's worse."

"I'm my own man!" Baston glared. The bandage on his arm and shoulder was filthy. "Nobody tells me what to do. Not even you!"

Con flushed and went to the bar. Slager set out a bottle.

Con asked where Dollop had managed to get his hands on enough money for a game with Charlie Baston.

"Claimed he lagged dollars with a drummer over at the hotel," Slager said. "Mebbe he did, I dunno."

"What's that supposed to mean?" Con said sharply.

"Well, it'll be the first time a drummer ever hit town an' didn't come to a saloon first thing for a drink."

"Well, maybe for once your brother-in-law has some gambling luck," Con said and looked around at the gaming table. But he couldn't see the players because of the crowd ringed around. "I hope he cleans Charlie. But I suppose that's too much to hope for."

Holding a glass, Con walked over and shouldered through the crowd. "You've got fifteen minutes, Charlie," he said. "Make up your mind to end it then."

Baston didn't even look up. The pot was large by postwar Texas standards, when a man could sell a Texas cow in Texas for maybe three dollars. And if he wanted to pay a debt with his Texas cows he might be lucky enough to charge off a dollar a head on the bill.

With a whoop of joy Charlie Baston raked in the chips. Dollop was broke. Shaken, the hotel clerk weaved over to the bar. "Barney, could you spare me a little? I feel my luck is changing. I honestly do."

Barney Slager scowled at his brother-in-law. "Go back and lag dollars with that drummer. Maybe you can win another two hundred dollars off him."

"Please, Barney. I feel—"

"You can drink my whisky. But none of my money for cards!"

Dollop drew himself up. "I don't have to take these insults! An ex-officer of the CSA, wounded in battle. I deserve some consideration."

"You get out, or you won't even get the whisky!"

Dollop, his head high, limped for the door.

When he was gone, Con said, "I'm surprised you put up with him, Barney."

"He married my wife's sister, God rest her soul. She took care of Mark while she was alive. I reckon she'd want me to look after him now that she's gone."

Con asked if Jud Kilhaven had been seen around town.

Then he asked about Bentley Hake. Slager said they had seen the man riding west on the stage road this morning.

"Damn fine man, Con," Slager said. "You've got a real man in that boss of yours."

"I wouldn't be too sure. And he isn't the only boss I have."

"Well," Slager said, "so far as I'm concerned, he's the only one who counts. I don't feel so bad about havin' a big cattle company own a Texas ranch now that I've seen, Hake."

"My feeling hasn't improved one damn bit."

Slager shrugged. "Imagine Hake and Arch Linnbrook in the war together. Arch never said much about the fightin' he done."

"I wish we had a jail here. I'd like to lock Arch up for about six months until he gets some loco notions out of his thick head."

"Arch is a damn thief, no mistake about that," Slager said confidentially. "Look at what he done to that pool herd last year."

"It's only gossip. Comanches *could* have been that far east."

"You know better'n that, Con."

"Whatever Arch has done is because of"—he was thinking of Nelda's reasoning— "the war. It changed a lot of things."

"If you ask me," Barney Slager went on, "his old man wasn't no better. He the same as stole Jawbone from you. If you ask me the whole Linnbrook tribe is rotten—"

"Careful, Barney," Con warned, and those nearest him at the bar jerked around, their faces tightening.

Slager spread his hands. "I'm sorry, Con. I—I never should've said that. I know how you feel about Nelda."

"And don't forget her mother. I owe that woman my life."

At that moment Mark Dollop returned. The hotel clerk's eyes were bright as he limped over to the table where Charlie Baston was arguing with Billy Snider. Dollop flung some gold pieces down on the gaming table.

"My luck has undergone a sudden change, Charlie," Dollop said, speaking with the stiffness of a man trying to sort his words out of the whisky vat that was his brain.

One hand was dealt for the money. And then came Charlie Baston's shout, "I never felt so rich in my life! Drinks on me, boys!"

And Ad Semple's thin voice cried, "Drink to the glory of Jefferson Davis."

Billy Snider, ruffling out his side whiskers, said sourly, "Ad, why not drink to the glory of our Mexican neighbors across the line?"

Ad Semple turned white and some men laughed. Con said, "Leave him alone." Then he walked over to the gaming table and looked down at Baston's face, a little pale now. "Charlie, we're going back to Doc Maxfield's."

"You ain't big enough to take me, one arm or not!" Baston shouted drunkenly.

Con sighed, remembering the other years with Charlie Baston and too much Texas cheer. It had been Poppa and Big Ed who handled him then.

Con said, "Charlie, you dropped a chip on the floor." And when Baston twisted around in his chair to stare down at the floor, Con hit him on the jaw.

Con enlisted the aid of two men to help him carry Baston. As they moved toward the door with him slung between them, Mark Dollop limped past. Con caught a glimpse of his face in a wedge of lamplight. He couldn't swear to it, but he thought Slager's brother-in-law was weeping.

When Charlie Baston was back in his bed at Doc Maxfield's, Con said, "He give you trouble, Doc?"

Doc Maxfield, smoking his pipe on the veranda, said wryly, "He has a tremendous wallop for a sick man." He rubbed the side of his face.

After thanking the pair who had helped him, Con walked back toward Slager's, intending to get his horse. At each alleyway he paused briefly and studied the shadows, a hand on his gun. The closeness of that bullet to his face out on the flats west of town last night was enough to put caution in a man.

As he reached the hitchrail he heard a girl call his name. Turning, he saw Coralee Whitley on the hotel veranda across the street. She wore her black dress and her hands seemed unusually white against the porch rail.

And her face seemed just as pale, he noted, as he stood

beside her on the veranda. "Can I be of service, Miss Whitley?"

"I—I wonder if you can help me. You understand I don't like to ask a favor. But Nelda spoke of you so often. And Arch—" She nervously bit her lip.

He felt an instant concern for this tall, pale-haired girl. "You've seen Arch?" he said, wondering if the reason for her agitation had something to do with the Linnbrook plans.

"No, I haven't seen Arch." Her voice was bitter. Then her gaze swept over his face. "Mr. Jason, I am supposed to leave on the morning stage—"

"Leave? But I thought you and Arch—"

"I've changed my mind about that."

"Then this is none of my affair," he said, and started away. She was just another fickle female, like Nelda, who would play with a man's feelings.

Lifting her hems, she hurried after him. "Mr. Jason—please."

He turned. Her blue eyes caught the reflection of the moon, held it. She was taller than Nelda. And her dress would equal anything he had seen at the Officer's Ball in Richmond when victory had seemed so near.

"My money," she whispered. "It's gone. I— You see, I left two hundred dollars with Mr. Dollop in an envelope which he put in the hotel safe. It was money Arch had forwarded so I could make this trip. I—I was returning it, together with a note."

"A note?"

"I didn't want Arch to think I looked on him with disfavor. It's just this country." She waved a slim white hand at the shadowed town. "This Texas. I couldn't live in a place like this."

"Arch plans his future in Chihuahua City."

"That would be even worse."

Con shook his head. "It's a fine city. I've been there."

She clenched her hands. "I understand there is no representative of the law in this town. So I am appealing to you. To help find the sneak thief who stole my money."

Con looked thoughtful for a moment, then glanced at the desk in the hotel lobby. There was no one behind it. "You can write for more money, can't you?" he said, facing her again. "Surely a woman of your position—"

"It was every cent I had in the world." She seemed close to tears.

"And you were going to return two hundred dollars of it to Arch Linnbrook?"

"It's only right that I repay him. As long as I don't intend to keep my end of the bargain by marrying him."

He shook his head slowly from side to side. "Your friend Nelda seems to think moral values disappeared with the war. I see that every female who attended that female academy in St. Louis doesn't share that viewpoint."

"Mr. Jason, I'm sure you'll be very happy with Nelda. Now if you would do me this one favor—I have no one else to turn to."

"How much did you lose? I mean in addition to the two hundred?"

She told him that she had kept one hundred and fifty dollars in her reticule. "I thought it would be enough to get me to Tucson."

"You believe the Territory of Arizona is a better place to live than Texas?"

"It couldn't be as bad. The stage passed a dead man on the way here. He was hanging by his neck and the vultures had—" She shuddered. "He had no face."

Con, his tone softer now, said, "If such things repel you, then I suggest a return to St. Louis."

"I have no one there. Nothing."

"Arizona won't be any better than Texas. We've taken land from the Apaches. They retaliate in uncivilized ways."

"That may be, but it is something I will have to learn in my own good time." There was strength in her voice, but with a shred of fear.

"You're trying very hard to be brave."

"I just want to get out of this town. I thought I could appeal to you. I don't know anyone else here but that Mr. Dollop. And he's drunk."

"You could get word to Arch."

"Can't you understand? I don't want to see him."

"Changed your mind about marriage just because you saw a dead man hanging?"

She shook her pale head and for a moment stared out onto the moon-swept street. "I changed my mind before I saw the dead man. Maybe it was the hard seat of the coach that did it. Discomfort makes a person aware of reality."

"And this made you aware of your feeling—or lack of it—for Arch?"

"I knew I was only marrying him for security. And I know there is no such thing."

For the first time in days a genuine smile touched his lips. "Coralee, I like you. Now let's talk about your money."

"Mr. Dollop said the hotel safe was robbed tonight. And the same thief broke into my room while I took the evening air here on the veranda."

"I had a feeling that's what happened," Con said, and with a fist hammered on Dollop's door behind the hotel desk. There was no answer, but he could hear someone's heavy breathing. Putting a shoulder to the door, he broke it open. Light from the lobby spilled across Dollop slumped on the bed.

"You and Charlie Baston," Con muttered, looking down at him. "You and Ad Semple. It seems all Texans can do these days is drink themselves out of their obligations. At least there's an excuse for Semple—his pride. An excuse for Charlie Baston this time—his pain. What's your excuse, Dollop?"

The man lay with an arm across his eyes. "I thought I could repay her double."

"You dirty sneak." He started to backhand Dollop across the face. The hotel clerk cringed. With an oath Con lowered his hand. "No wonder we lost the war if we had to rely on men like you."

Dollop lay there, his eyes sick.

"You've left that girl stranded," Con said harshly. "Now you listen to me. You've bragged that you're a Confederate hero. Act like one. She's going to have that money back by morning, understand. One way or another.

There was the sound of a hard-ridden horse in the street and then a voice—Jake Deward's by the sound of it— "Con! Con Jason!"

A premonition of disaster touching him, Con rushed out. Coralee stood tensely on the veranda. In front of Slager's the black-bearded Deward was just swinging down. Con patted the girl's arm, told her, he'd be back in a minute. Then he hurried across the street just as Deward was about to enter Slager's.

"Here I am, Jake," Con said. "What's up?"

"Them thousand head of cows on the mesa," Deward said, panting for breath after the long ride. "They're gone. Ever' damn head."

Men had come out of Slager's to see what the trouble was but Con said nothing. He and Deward rode out of town. A mile from Santa Margarita he remembered Coralee Whitley. He couldn't turn back now. She'd just have to stay around a little longer. The prospect was pleasing.

They had been pushing their horses and now Con gave the signal to slow up. "I didn't want to talk back there in town, Jake. Never know who's got the long ear. I even sent Timoteo clear over to San Pablo to mail some letters. All right, now tell me about the rustlers."

"Arch is with 'em."

"I guessed as much," Con said, his voice hardening. "You sent the boys after the cows?"

Deward fingered his eyepatch a moment. The moon was climbing. "It's kinda ticklish business, Con."

"In what way?"

"You and Arch— Well, if we went after 'em and there was a fight and Arch got killed. You wouldn't feel kindly toward them that done it."

For a moment Con was tempted to tell Deward that a thief was a thief, whether you'd been raised with him or not. And then he thought of a long ride through drenching rain twenty-five years ago. A newborn infant wrapped in a serape, carried by Timoteo. And then Mrs. Linnbrook giving life to the infant. Con swallowed.

"Maybe it's better this way, Jake. I'll try and have a talk with Arch. I'll give him one chance to get back on the right side of the creek. If he doesn't—" Con broke off, staring at the distant winking of light from Jawbone headquarters. "Well, it's up to Arch."

They stopped at Jawbone for fresh horses, then rode on. At sunup they came to the camp on the mesa where Con's men were bunched. They looked sour. Con ate the breakfast

Sam Trench cooked for him. The food lay in his stomach
like stones from the river. Putting his plate aside, Con rolled
a cigarette and looked at the silent crew.

"Something on your mind, boys?" he asked.

The lank Sam Trench scowled, glanced around at the
others, then said, "You got to understand how we feel, Con.
If it was anybody but—"

"You mean you don't want to ride against Arch?" He
touched a brand to his cigarette, dropped it back into the
cookfire. "I'm having a talk with Arch."

"It ain't that," Sam Trench said uneasily.

Jake Deward said, "You got to understand, Con. It was
some different when your pa and Big Ed was alive. We
stretched some necks in those days. Because the cows that
was stole belonged to Jawbone."

"These cows still belong to Jawbone."

Dave Rubel, his round boyish face serious for once, had
come up. "These here is Yankee cows, Con."

Con's nerves were jumping from the pressures he'd been
under these past hours. He whirled on the younger man. He
was about to cuss Rubel out, then he muttered, "What the
hell. You don't understand." He looked around. "None of
you understand."

"If you still owned Jawbone, Con," Deward said, "it
would—"

But Con cut him off. "Sure, I know they're Yankee-owned
cows. But isn't there such a thing as integrity left in Texas?
Are we going to let the fact that we lost a war turn us into
a pack of animals?"

"You don't see how it is, Con," Sam Trench said uneasily.

"We condone theft," Con said, "because it's stealing from
former enemies. Forgetting we draw the pay of these men."

"I ain't proud of drawin' their pay," Jake Deward put in."

Con turned on the one-eyed man, his gaze furious. "Then
if you've got so much pride. Why in hell don't you quit?"

Deward flushed. There was an uncomfortable silence in
camp. "We all figured to stick as long as you needed us,"
Deward said.

"I still need you." Con looked around at the silent faces
of these men he had ridden with so long. "Jake, I'm sorry I
blew off at you. But—"

"Con, I don't hold with a rustler no more'n the next man," Sam Trench said. "But damn if I can see mebbe killin' a neighbor just to keep some Yankee cows from endin' up in Mexico."

"If Alliance goes broke you're out of a job."

"It ain't easy for a man my age to get on with anybody for a ridin' job," Sam Trench said seriously. "But even so it don't change my mind none about how I feel."

Con turned and looked across the mesa with its shin oak and the towering pines and junipers. He felt his frustrations as he had in the war. How many times had he witnessed the blunder of the Federals during the conflict? But always something happened to counteract it. The brilliant strategy of Lee could not long withstand the steamroller wave of blue once it got started after the bungling at Gettysburg. And from that time on had come the certainty that the war was lost. He could even understand his father and Big Ed making that last defiant gesture against a Yankee field piece. A man runs for just so long and then he turns.

And here it was again. This land where he had been raised. Everything gone wrong, as it had for Lee at Gettysburg. It had started with Bert Linnbrook selling the notes on Jawbone —a traitorous act to a fellow-Texan. But Con even overlooked that—or tried to—because of his ties to the other Linnbrooks.

Con turned to his men, his mind struggling for some means to make them see the light.

But Billy Snider came riding in then. The gaunt rancher with the white sideburns was leading a black horse with a Chihuahua saddle.

"Was on my way home," Billy Snider said to the silent Jawbone men. "Figured to ride over here to the mesa an' see if any of you boys was around."

"Where'd you find him, Billy?"

"Pacheco Creek, south of the Dome."

Con swallowed and Sam Trench said, "That's the south boundary of the Linnbrook place."

Jake Deward brushed a hand over his black beard. "You said you sent Timoteo to San Pablo, Con."

"I did." Con walked over and examined horse and saddle.

There was no blood on it. "Thanks, Billy," he said. "We'll take over."

Billy Snider dropped the reins of the black horse. "You reckon the old Mex got throwed?"

"Not Timoteo," Con said, white about the mouth. "That old man could stick to a greased mule in a Blue Norther."

"What you reckon happened to him, then?"

"I intend finding out," Con said crisply. And when Snider rode out, heading for his two-bit spread over east, Con turned to his men. "I suppose if we find the old man with a Texas bullet in his back it'll be all right. Just so the slug didn't come from a Yankee gun."

"We'll go with you, Con," Deward said.

"Take Timoteo's horse. Get back to headquarters. I'm going alone."

He rode west, and he brushed a hand over his saddle rope. He hoped it wouldn't be Arch Linnbrook's neck that would fit the noose.

Chapter Eleven

AS SOON AS the herd was moving toward the river, Arch told Kilhaven he was going to town. He didn't wait for Kilhaven to give him any argument. Hurrying northward, he kept his eyes open for Jawbone riders. But he didn't see any. He intended seeing Coralee. And by God, nobody was going to stop him. Hake or nobody else.

Even when he was some distance from town Arch knew there was trouble ahead. He could see dust and the breeze carried an occasional shout. Sweating a little, he checked the loads of his gun, shoved it back in the holster and rode in.

There was a crowd milling about between Slager's and the Monument Hotel. Arch saw that two men held a screaming Ad Semple by the arms. Another man hit Semple in the face.

Doc Maxfield saw Arch at the edge of the crowd and rushed up, the stem of a cold pipe clenched in his teeth. "Maybe you can stop this madness, Arch!" the doctor cried.

Arch swung down, feeling a coldness in his legs. "What

in hell's goin' on, Doc?" There were many possibilities. The shouting increased and a coil of rope went sailing over the heads of the crowd. A man snatched it up and Arch saw a noose dropped over Ad Semple's head.

Doc Maxfield stood on tiptoe, trying to shout into Arch's ear. Arch had to bend down to hear him because of all the noise.

"They found Timoteo's body west of town about an hour ago!"

"The hell you say," Arch said, swallowing. There were a few sunbonneted women on the walks. One of them screaming for her young son to "Git away afore you git trampled!"

Doc went on, his bald head red as his face now, "They found Timoteo mutilated and——"

"What you mean by that?" Arch demanded, looking down.

"It's the same thing the Mexicans did to Ad Semple years ago," Doc Maxfield said. And then he added, "You remember. Seeing Ad's scars, so to speak, is what put the fear of God in you and Ed Jason and some of the other young bucks around here."

"You mean somebody cut Timoteo?" Arch shook his head, trying to figure this one out.

"Because of that they're sure Ad Semple killed him. You know, Ad's hatred of the Mexicans. Ad wouldn't kill anybody. Come on, Arch." Doc Maxfield had a hand on his arm, tugging him along. "You can talk sense to these maniacs."

Reluctantly Arch went along. And then he glanced toward the hotel and saw Coralee on the veranda, her face white. He lifted a hand to her. But because of the crowd she likely didn't see him. Anyway she gave no indication.

Ad Semple, spittle running over his chin, saw Arch. "Help me, Arch. You drunk whisky with me many times for the glory of the Rebellion. I wouldn't kill the old Mex."

Barney Slager, his face hard under the brush of pale hair, said, "Ad, you hated every Mexican that ever drew breath."

"Sure—sure I did." Ad Semple's eyes were pleading now. "But I never killed him."

Arch tried to lick some moisture into his lips. He glanced over his shoulder, saw Coralee still on the porch. He wanted to go over and speak to her and tell her he was sorry he hadn't

been able to get to town sooner. But now he was trapped
with this crazy business of Timoteo and Ad Semple.

Doc Maxfield said, "You men listen to reason now. The
law should—"

"You got to do some ridin' to get to the law in these
parts," Barney Slager said. "I figure we'll be our own law,
Doc."

Doc said, looking up at the towering Arch Linnbrook,
"You're the biggest man here. And you're wearing a gun.
Stop this thing, Arch. You can do it."

Desperately Arch tried in his slow mind to figure out what
had happened. How did Ad Semple get into this, the simple
killing of a man for his horse and gun? At least that was what
Kilhaven had claimed. And he'd been riding Timoteo's
horse. With Timoteo's saddle on it. And they had turned the
horse loose down by Pacheco Creek. Just what in hell was
this all about?

Barney Slager said, "Ad is guilty as hell."

"No!" Ad Semple screamed. Tears ran down his face and
along the creases in his fat neck.

"Who else would cut a man like that?" Slager said, his
gaze hot on the trembling man with the rope around his neck.

Doc Maxfield shouldered up. "Ad, tell us just what
happened?"

There were shouts of protest. "We *know* what happened!"

But Doc held up his hands for silence, which did no good.
Somebody gave a tug on the rope and Ad Semple went to
one knee. He clawed at the noose around his neck. Doc
looked up at Arch again.

And Arch bellowed, "Wait a minute!" And when the
shouting had subsided, he said, "All right, Ad. Speak your
piece."

It took Semple a moment before his voice stopped shaking
long enough for anybody to make sense out of what he tried
to say. Semple said he'd seen buzzards over west of his
shack and he'd walked over.

"I seen this dead hoss. Wearin' a Four T brand," Semple
said, his lips trembling.

Arch stiffened. Kilhaven's horse. Sweet Mother of God!

Semple went on, "Then I seen more buzzards. And I cut
over about a quarter mile an' there was the dead Mex."

"And then you cut him!" Arch said.

"No. I never."

"Tell the truth, Ad," Doc Maxfield said sternly. "It's your only chance."

"God's truth," Ad Semple said, and began to weep.

Doc Maxfield said, "This story is strange," and he looked around at the men who had quieted now. "What would Timoteo be doing on a Four T horse? He rides that big black."

Harvey Pearce, the fat hostler, spoke up. "I recollect that *segundo* out at Jawbone ridin' a hoss with that brand. He was in last week. Jud Kilhaven."

Arch felt a chill in his entrails. Rustling was one thing, but getting mixed up in a thing like this . . .

Doc Maxfield stepped rght up to Ad Semple and looked the man in the eye. "You're holding something back, Ad."

Before Semple could answer, Arch said quickly, "I figure we heard enough."

Doc Maxfield turned on him. "As Con Jason's friend, you should be vitally interested in learning the truth. Con will be some broken up. As if he'd lost his own father." And then Doc Maxfield added, "More so, as a matter of fact."

Ad Semple, drying his tears on the sleeve of his shirt, suddenly sagged against the men who gripped his arms. "All right," he said, his head down. "I cut him. But he was already dead. I figured it sorta made up for what they done to me."

There was a grave silence instead of shouts. The men looked at each other. Barney Slager nodded. "He admits usin' the knife. He killed the old man, all right. Let's go, boys."

They marched the screaming Ad Semple down to the livery stable, leaving Arch Linnbrook and Doc Maxfield alone in the street.

"They'll hang him to a rafter," Doc Maxfield said. "You could still stop it."

"You stop it, if you're a mind to."

"They'd pay no attention to me. But they would to you. I'd have to take a gun and kill every one of them."

Arch turned his back and walked into the deserted saloon. He walked behind the bar and got a bottle and worked the

cork out with his teeth. He could still hear Ad Semple
screaming. And suddenly the screams stopped.

Arch took a long drink, and another. The whisky only
intensified the deep shame in him. But he tried to tell himself
that Ad Semple's life had been over since that day years ago
when some Mexicans had caught him along the river after
finding one of their women naked and screaming in the brush.

But the shame was like a cold wedge of steel in him.
Driving deeper into his entrails.

Woodenly he went outside. The men were coming out of
the livery barn now, talking in low tones. From the livery
came a great shrilling of horses. Excited by the thing hanging
there—

Arch went to the hotel and looked around for Coralee.
He didn't see her. But he looked in the register, saw the
number of her room and climbed the stairs. He knocked on
the door. "Coralee."

"Go away, Arch," she sobbed. "I never want to see you
again as long as I live."

He tried again, but she refused to speak to him. Hands in
his pockets, he went downstairs and out into the alley behind
the hotel. He wanted to be alone for a few moments. He
didn't want to go out into the street or into Slager's and
listen to them tell what they had done to Ad Semple. He
wanted to think. He wanted to get the tangle out of his mind.
What was happening to him? He was all snarled up like a
calf in a loose rope.

And that girl inside telling him she never wanted to see
him again. That girl he had loved since the day he had stood
awkwardly in a big house in St. Louis and she had smiled
at him.

He crossed the alley, his boots kicking through the dust.
He passed a shed and something caught his attention. Wheeling, he pushed a hand for his gun. Slowly he dropped his
hand when he saw what it was.

Mark Dollop was sitting on the ground, slumped over, his
back against the shed. The butt of a small revolver was
wedged between Dollop's face and the dusty ground. Between
the hotel clerk's clenched teeth was the barrel of the gun.
The back of his head had been splattered over the shed wall.

Feeling sick, Arch strode for his horse. He'd had enough

death for one day. Let somebody else discover Dollop's body. He rode south, toward the river. He had to tell Hank and Kilhaven about this business of Semple. And Jud's horse being found. He didn't give a damn about Jud Kilhaven's neck. But he didn't want Con to ever find out that he, Arch Linnbrook, knew the details of Timoteo's death and had done nothing about it. Because if this happened he knew he would have to kill Con Jason or be killed.

He wished now he'd listened to Con. This whole business had blown higher than a July moon. It all went back to the war. He had become scarred in many ways. And he knew with a sure male instinct that his own sister bore her scars. He knew there had been someone in St. Louis but she would never tell him. He hoped Con never found out.

"Why didn't I listen to the old man?" he said with a catch in his throat.

On his deathbed Bert Linnbrook had said, "We need Con Jason in this family. Somebody strong. You and Nelda are weaklings."

And Arch had hated his father for saying that. But he had to admit that the old man had known what he was talking about.

But it was too late for ary of these things the old man wished for. Arch wished mightily he had never laid eyes on Bentley Hake.

Chapter Twelve

CON FOUND WHERE Timoteo's horse had been with a bunch moving south. The other horses had been ridden. So he back-tracked the horses and felt a coldness in his stomach as he approached 88.

He rode in. The yard was deserted, the bunkhouse door hanging open. One corral was empty. The other held six head of horses. Bert Linnbrook had built his house so that the front windows overlooked cottonwoods and not the outbuildings.

He rode around in front and saw Nelda sitting stiffly in the hardwood rocker her father had used for so many years. She wore a cotton dress that had shrunk with washing. The straining of her breasts had ripped it along one side. Her green eyes watched him, a little fearfully he thought.

Swinging down, Con climbed to the porch. The front door was ajar. He started to look into the house. But Nelda said, "You've come back to ask my forgiveness?"

He looked around. Her smile was pale and after a moment she laughed. "It seems that I don't have much luck. With you." She got up and glanced at the door. "Luck with anything."

"Who's inside?" he demanded quietly, nodding at the house.

"Jefferson Davis," she said, her lips twisted. "Who do you think?"

An angry flush touched her face. And for the first time in the unkind sunlight he saw a dryness about her mouth with its incipient lines of age and discontent. She pushed at her dark-red hair.

"You're a fool, Con," she said, leaning forward. "An idealist. Your own father said so once."

"I'm not surprised."

"Trading a Jawbone horse to a frightened Abolitionist running for his life. Trading for a wagonload of books."

"My father took care of that. He burned the books for me."

"And he hanged the Abolitionist."

For a moment he stared at her, trying to remember the girl he had known before the war. "Nelda, what's happened?"

"Nothing."

He stood a moment, then he sauntered over and put his back to the house wall and drew his gun. "Tell whoever is in there to step out."

"You have no right to order me in my own house—"

"Timoteo's dead. His horse was here."

"One of the men found it," she said looking him in the eye, "wandering by the stage road. He brought it in."

"Then what happened?"

She shrugged. "Arch and some of the others took it south with them. Didn't he stop by your place?"

"No."

Reaching around the door frame, Con pushed the door wider and said, "All right. Come out with your hands up."

There was a sudden tinkling of glass behind him. Con spun, saw the twin barrels of a shotgun jutting through the broken window. Saw Bentley Hake's face, his tight smile.

"Throw your gun into the yard," Hake ordered.

Con stood there, seeing the fear in Nelda's eyes. And something else there. Was it shame? And behind her was Hake with the shotgun. Only a portion of his face visible because of the angle of the window. One blast from that gun could kill every living thing on that porch.

Carefully Con lifted his gun and threw it over the porch railing. It landed in the yard, raising a small puff of dust.

He looked at Nelda. "Is this what you call rebound?"

She said nothing, just stood with her hands clenched.

Con looked down at the warped planks of the porch, scuffed by the hard boots of many men. Boots worn by his own father and his brother. Con's first pair of man boots hard against this porch when he came to call on the girl who had been promised since her birth.

Slowly Hake raised the window and stepped out on the porch. He came to stand beside Nelda. She flushed. The flush extended down her throat and darkened the shadow between her breasts.

Hake's white shirt was wilted. He needed a shave. His boots were covered with dust. "I could end everything right now," he said, the shotgun pointed at Con's stomach.

Nelda said, "No. You promised. When we saw him riding in, you said there would be no shooting."

Hake's dark eyes were bloodshot. "What about it, Jason? Does a man's promise to a woman mean anything in this country?"

"I'm gambling you won't commit a cold-blooded murder."

"It's been done."

"Probably," Con said, keeping his voice level. "Timoteo, one of the Jawbone hands is missing. I'll find out what happened to him."

Deliberately he turned his back and walked down the steps. He thought he heard Nelda give a sharp, forlorn cry as he rode away. He wasn't sure, and it did not interest him sufficiently to turn his head.

Only when he was out of the yard did the tension go out of his back. It was drenched with sweat. There had been the chance that Hake would cut loose with the shotgun.

Con turned his horse toward town. There he would get another revolver. This was no time for a man to have only his rifle. With storm clouds boiling up over the Bend it was the time for a man to have a short gun in case he had to come in close to a man. And kill him up close.

In his mind's eye he saw Arch Linnbrook, shouting as he had when they were boys. Going to the river to fish. And Nelda—

It was all gone now. Everything was gone.

When Con had gone and there was only a tracery of dust to mark his passage from 88, Bentley Hake lowered the shotgun. "I didn't know whether your friend Jason would bluff or not," he said. "Or if I cared very much either way."

"He bluffed only so I wouldn't be hurt," Nelda said.

"You think he's still in love with you?"

"No."

Hake looked faintly amused. "You're a fool, Nelda. But then most women are."

Nelda gave him a fiery green-eyed stare. "Thanks for the objective view."

"You should have kept me dangling, so to speak."

"Just what does that mean?" she demanded.

"You find a challenging mountain," Hake said, giving her his handsome smile. "And you climb it. But there's not much point in making another ascent. The challenge is gone."

"I see."

"And so is the novelty gone."

Her lips twisted. "Don Juan in Texas," she said.

"It's a way of life. Just what did Jud do to you so that you hate him so much?"

"I didn't say I hated him."

"You claimed you overheard him plotting to shoot me in the back."

"I did. But it doesn't matter now."

"No, it doesn't." Leaning the shotgun against the wall he fired up a cheroot. "Among other things, you're a liar, Nelda. The last thing in the world Jud Kilhaven would ever do is shoot me in the back. We've taken different names, but the blood's the same. We're brothers."

"Two snakes under the same rock."

His hand flashed against her face, snapping back her head. She fell against the porch rail and went to one knee, skinning it. She glared at him.

He said, no longer smiling, "I'll have a talk with Jud. I want to know why you concocted such a story about him. But I can guess. Brother or not I don't care to wallow in the pasture he's been treading."

"If I had a gun," she said, her voice shaking, "I'd kill you."

Later she stood on the porch, watching him ride south. He wore his dark coat, his hat slanted against the glare of the sun. She felt old and withered and for a moment she wondered just how far the slugs from a shotgun would carry. But she knew it would be no use to try to find out. Of course he would have unloaded the weapon and put the shells where she would not be able to find them easily.

Chapter Thirteen

AT THE MERCANTILE, Con picked up a revolver and soberly listened to the story of Ad Semple. And Timoteo. Then he went to Slager's, where he found some of his men looking somber. Word had been awaiting them at Jawbone when they pulled in. Timoteo's body had been found.

Barney Slager went into detail about the hanging of Ad Semple. And when he had finished, Con looked across the bar at him. "A damn fine bunch of men you are," he said loudly, so that talk in the barroom ceased. "Ad didn't kill Timoteo."

And when Con started to curse him, Sam Trench, standing at his elbow, said, "Barney's havin' his own grief. His brother-in-law shot himself sometime last night."

Con drank off his whisky and stood looking at the wet marks on the bar. For hours he had suspected that Timoteo lay dead somewhere. This second passing had not been expected. But perhaps under the circumstances it was better for Dollop, better for the town. If suicide could ever be condoned, that is.

"Well, Dollop was a Confederate hero, anyhow," Jake Deward said.

"Maybe I shouldn't say this about him, now that he's gone," Slager said, his heavy face a little sad. "But he was only an errand boy around Jeff Davis' headquarters. One night he got drunk and a dray run him down. He limped ever since."

"Just the same," Jake Deward said defensively, "he wore gray. Makes him one of us. How about that, Con?"

Con raised his glass. "One of us." And he thought, Dollop put a gun in his mouth and murdered himself. Because he could no longer stand himself. I wonder how it'll be with Arch, when he finally comes face to face with Arch Linnbrook and his stomach turns sour at the sight of him.

"Barney, I can't spare any riders," Con said to the saloonman. "Can you send somebody to San Pablo?"

Barney Slager's eyes were veiled. "Reckon. Why?"

"I want to get word to the sheriff that we need help here."

"A letter might do better," Slager said.

"I wrote a letter," Con said bitterly. "I wrote several letters. With Timoteo dead it's a damn cinch they never were mailed."

Slager shook his head. "Likely won't do no good. Yankees got most to say about law over that way now. If we got trouble here they won't give much of a damn. They'll likely cheer."

"Send somebody, Barney. I want you boys as witnesses," Con added, turning to the men ranged along the bar, "that I tried to get word. I don't want that San Pablo bunch to come down here when it's over and count the headstones. And say 'Why weren't we notified there was trouble?'"

Slager rubbed his heavy jaw. "I'll see if I can get somebody to ride over."

"And spread the word I can use some men."

"Might take some doin' to get anybody to fight to save Yankee cows," Slager said.

"There's Timoteo to avenge. I may have to shoot my way through a damn big pack of men to get at who killed him."

"Ad Semple done it—" Slager dropped his gaze from Con's

hot eyes. "Timoteo was a white man. White as any of us—"

"You don't have to make a point of it, Barney," Con said coldly. "The skin means nothing. White is the color of a man's heart. At least a man like Timoteo."

"You figure to bury him tonight?"

"At Jawbone. He spent most of his life there." Con's voice broke.

Con crossed the street to the hotel, looking for Coralee. But he couldn't find her. One of the loafers in the lobbby said she had been seen riding out of town. The hanging of Ad Semple had shaken her up, the man said.

"When she comes back," Con said, "ask her to stay here. Say that I'll take care of a certain matter for her."

He went outside and walked toward a shed behind the livery, his men trailing along silently. He knew he should speak to Slager about the money stolen from Coralee. But he didn't feel like bringing it up on the day the thief had killed himself. Especially when he was a relative of sorts of Slager's.

On the shed floor three bodies were laid out; Semple, Mark Dollop and Timoteo.

They claimed their own and rode out with it.

Despite his bad shoulder, Charlie Baston had been out of bed most of the day. He was drunk, barely able to sit his saddle. Damned if he'd miss the funeral of an old friend, he said.

Con knew it was useless to argue with him.

Behind the Jawbone barn, with the moon strong and the wind stirring the cottonwoods, Con felt a sting of tears as he stared into the rectangular cut in the earth. And saw the hard pine lid of the box that would temporarily at least seal off the empty shell of a man who had lived.

"Ashes to ashes—" The hard thunk of clods striking the boards, the mound of earth. The headboard carved in a plank torn from a barn wall, the dates incomplete because no one knew exactly how old he had been:

TIMOTEO SANCHEZ
18—   1867

Con blew his nose and stared into the darkness. He wished in a way he had never come back to Texas after the war. But can a man flee tragedy no matter where he tries to hide? he asked himself.

And even greater tragedy was coming. A sickness grew in him as he thought of it. The war had been bad enough but that had been impersonal to an extent. You fought a uniform, not a man. But the death that would sweep the Bend was not impersonal. There would be other men buried in the hard Texas earth and each time a shovelful of dirt struck a coffin lid a little of you would also die.

Jake Deward came up behind Con and said quietly, "There's somebody yonder in them cottonwoods." He nodded toward the trees that threw a great shadow beyond the west side of the house.

"I'll take a look," Con said grimly. "You keep me covered."

Chapter Fourteen

EARLIER IN THE day Arch Linnbrook had arrived at Vega Verde across the river. There were six shacks made of willow poles, a corral and a great circle of rocks covered by sheet iron. Beneath the iron the cookfire had burned down to ash. A monte game was in progress on an Indian blanket in the shade of some willows. There were some twenty-five men at the rustler hangout. Some of them cleaned their weapons, others watched the monte game. They were a hard-faced, taciturn lot, each man with a belt gun and holding a rifle.

Arch Linnbrook's crew, what was left of it, was here. Leacham seemed unhappy. He came over while Arch got himself a drink from an *olla*.

"Wish we'd get to movin'," Leacham said; the lines in his face were caked with dust. "A man thinks too much when he's settin' around."

Arch told him about the business in town. How Timoteo's body had been found and the hanging of Ad Semple.

"You never should've let 'em stretch ol' Ad's neck," Leacham said.

"Better they stretched mine?" Arch snapped.

"You never killed Timoteo. Kilhaven done it." His gaze swung toward the lank Kilhaven, who stood some distance away watching the monte game.

Arch walked over. "Where's Hake?"

"Still up at your place, I reckon." Kilhaven's muddy brown eyes were thin. He rubbed the swollen place on his jaw where Arch had struck him.

"Why would he still be there?" Arch demanded.

"Mebbe he's got somethin' pleasurable to do."

Laughing, Kilhaven moved away. Arch watched him for a moment, his gaze hard. Then clenching his big hands, Arch walked beyond the shacks where he could see the thousand head of Jawbone beef spread out on the flats, surrounded by the dun-colored hills. This would be used as a holding ground and when the rest of the Jawbone cows were brought down here the entire herd would be pushed south and west to Chihuahua.

With the hot wind of Mexico in his face, Arch was reminded of another day, when the heat seared a man's cheeks and his throat was so constricted it seemed that he had been trying to swallow string all day. It was in Kansas where the remnants of gray were gathering and there was talk of joining up with Shelby. But this never materialized simply because at the time there was no direction, no purpose. Only survival. And Arch knew he owed his life to the renegade Captain Hake, escaped from a Union stockade near Chicago. Also in the group was Jud Kilhaven, late of Quantrill's raiders, wounded and left behind. And with Kilhaven, his friend Homer Peale.

It was Bentley Hake's daring that enabled them to outwit the Federal patrols sent to round them up. They lived off the land, sometimes brutally.

Eventually they crossed into Missouri and with the ending of the war they melted into the brawling metropolis of St. Louis. There Hake had connections and one day he appeared in new broadcloth and carrying a gold-headed cane. He had been with old friends, the Whitleys. "The old man is an unregenerate Rebel, Arch. He lost heavily in the war. But he has one steamer left. It carries four thousand rifles, a hundred thousand rounds of ammunition, four field pieces and ball. We'll run the river blockade and make our way to Mexico.

Shelby will fight on there. The war isn't over, my friend."

"I've got a Texas ranch. My pa is old. And Nelda's livin'
back there now—"

"As an inducement for you to think about staying," Hake
interrupted, "the Whitleys have a daughter, Coralee. It
shows the smallness of the world when I mentioned your
name. She went to school here with Nelda. She wants to see
you and inquire after your sister's health."

In a big rambling house with oaken doors and broad
verandas Arch met Coralee. The slave quarters were empty,
the silver service sold. And Coralee, apparently not minding
Arch's ill-fitting clothes, his frontier awkwardness, said
"Nelda spoke of you so often. When are you going to see
her?"

Arch was about to say he was joining Shelby in Mexico,
but Hake shook his dark head in warning. And while they
were dining a messenger arrived with grave news. The
Whitley steamer had blown up at dockside, with Coralee's
father dead from the shock. His heart. Mrs. Whitley fainted
at the table and her corsets had to be loosened before she was
carried upstairs. She survived only a short time.

The grand plans for the resumption of the war on Mexican
soil died so far as Arch was concerned. He returned to Texas.
Whenever Nelda wrote Coralee, he enclosed a note of his
own.

The following spring Arch decided to gamble because he
had no money. He formed a cattle pool, some beef of his
own and a hundred head each from some of the small Bend
ranchers. He had written Coralee of his plans and told her
he hoped to see her in St. Louis when the herd was sold.

He was not surprised when he met Bentley Hake on the
trail. Because Coralee had written that Hake was back in
St. Louis and that she had mentioned the fact that Arch was
coming north again.

With light from a campfire strong against the sky Hake
told of his new connection. While a prisoner of war in
Chicago, he had made friends. And these friends had proved
to be invaluable; they needed someone who knew the cattle
business. And they had picked up the notes on Jawbone, and
things were looking bright because Arch's neighbor and
friend, Con Jason, had been retained as manager-foreman.

"I have some plans of my own," Hake said, "to be disclosed at the proper time. We can use your friend Jason. Always bear in mind that the war isn't over. The Yankees are still our enemies.

Arch left his man and his herd and went with Hake to a place on the river where there was a plank bar and music and girls with bright mouths. In the morning Arch woke up with a head big as Texas and a vow never to touch whisky again.

But he was even sicker when Hake showed him a bill-of-sale for the cattle herd. And there was Arch's signature on the document. The herd lost on the turn of a card, Hake said.

"Don't you even remember wanting to bet with me, old friend?" Hake said..

"I don't remember one damn thing."

"Millie said you were pretty drunk, but—"

"Who in the hell is Millie?"

Hake looked at him with some surprise. "I guess you *were* drunk."

Because Arch was his friend, Hake said, he passed back five hundred dollars in gold coins. "No use letting your Texas neighbors know you gambled away their cows. Take the five hundred and tell them that Indians jumped the herd."

But there was the crew to consider and this was taken care of by Arch firing the lot of them. And a couple who protested became located permanently under the Missouri sod. In time some of the crew drifted back to Texas and the story spread like dust flung into the air that Arch Linnbrook was a damn thief.

But nobody made an issue of it because aside from a recognized ability with a gun, Arch was known as a talented brawler. In his twenty-five years he had left men dead from bullets as well as his fists.

Leacham, who had stayed behind to run 88 was the only old-timer left on the payroll.

"I don't care how I make it," Arch told Bentley Hake as they parted company in Missouri. "I want money. The war ruined Texas. It'll never be worth more'n forty cents an acre. If we had any sense we'd give it back to the Mexicans an' let them suffer with it."

"Speaking of Mexicans," Hake had said, "I have a friend who is a cattle buyer in Chihuahua City."

"Where *ain't* you got friends?"

Hake smiled at this, obviously flattered. "I make a business of being personable. Of being able to tip certain individuals to means of profit whether they be Rebel or Yankee. Amazing how many friends you have when you can show them how to make money."

"Seems like since the war everybody's a thief at heart."

"Since the first war in history, Arch. Since the day when our ancestors first took stone clubs to the skulls of their neighbors. We've been thieves ever since. Because winning a war brings out the thieves and then we fight a bigger war to undo the mischief caused by the previous one."

"I don't follow all this," Arch said, shaking his head, "but I guess you know what you're doin'."

"Stick on my saddle blanket like a bur and I may dance at your wedding in Chihuahua City."

Arch, looking at the Jawbone cattle today, horns flashing in the Mexican sunlight, wondered morosely if there would ever be a wedding in Chihuahua City.

Chapter Fifteen

WITH DRAWN GUN Con walked down to the cottonwoods beyond the house, where the shadows were deep and the moonlight did not penetrate. A slim boy stepped out of the trees and came toward him. The boy wore a flat-crowned hat and a dark shirt and pants narrow in the leg.

But the voice did not belong to a boy. "Mr. Jason—"

He holstered the gun when she came up. "Coralee Whitley," he said. "How long have you been out here?"

"I—I had to get away from that town. When you didn't come to try and help me. I came to you."

"I did promise to help, and I will."

He saw her shoulders contract as if she might be taken with a chill. "That awful town, the things that happened there today."

"It wasn't pleasant," he agreed. "But you shouldn't have ridden out here at night."

It was daylight when she left, she explained, but she got lost and the livery stable horse she had rented turned up lame. She tied the reins to the saddle horn and he limped back in the direction of town. "I was lost, but I saw lights over this way," she said. "It seems like I've been walking for hours."

"You're lucky it was lights from Jawbone that you saw."

"I—I was hiding in the trees when you rode in. Was it a burial?"

"Yeah," he said, his voice hard. "A burial."

"I'm so sorry. I thought it was, but I couldn't be sure because of the dark. I thought it best if I didn't interfere."

"So many things have happened," he told her, "I neglected to get your money back." He noticed a smudge of dirt on her cheek, then added, "I guess Dollop just got tired of living with himself."

"I hope he didn't kill himself because of that money he stole from me."

"Probably contributed," Con said, and let his gaze touch the boy's shirt that fit her too snugly across the chest.

"Maybe I could work in the hotel dining room until I get enough money for my passage to Arizona," she said.

"I promised to help you and I will," he said curtly. "You don't have to try and pressure me into it by talking about a job."

She drew back, peering up at him. "But I would work. Why not?"

"This isn't St. Louis, Miss Whitley—"

"I'm quite aware of that fact," she said. "If you will loan me a horse I'll go back to town. I was frightened and lonely and upset over what happened in Santa Margarita. I'm sorry I bothered you."

"I'm sorry," he said. "So much has happened—" He lifted a hand, let it fall. "I just thought you were trying to gain my sympathy. By saying you'd work in the hotel."

"But I would. If they had a job for me. Do you think I'm above such work?"

"I know somebody who is." He was thinking of Nelda.

"You impressed me when we talked in town. I should have remembered you're a young lady not afraid to face life."

He tried to lead her toward the house, but she hung back, biting her lip. "I think that under the circumstances I should return to town. My nerves are quite settled now."

He let a weary smile touch his lips. "You can stay at the house until we plan something. I'll sleep in the bunkhouse. I'm hungry, are you?"

"Yes," she admitted.

He took her to the house, then went down to the cookshack and asked Sam Trench to cook up some steaks. Then he got the black-bearded Jake Deward aside.

"Jake, post guards," Con ordered. "Two shots if there's trouble."

Deward spat tobacco juice against the wall of the shed where he was standing. He glanced at the house, then looked at Con. "You still fixin' to marry with Arch's sister?"

"I don't know anyone named Arch. I don't know his sister." He nodded toward 88. "Those people over there are strangers."

"Makes it easier to shoot a gun in his face, or hang him if you figure it's a stranger you're doin' it to?"

"Maybe." He put a hand on Deward's shoulder, and the man's good eye watched him. "We need more men, Jake. But if we can't get them we'll go after the beef Hake has stolen."

"If Arch had a hand in killin' Timoteo some way," Deward said, "I can cut out his heart an' smile while I'm doin' it. But—" Deward let his voice trail away.

"But not the cattle, is that it?" Con demanded. "You won't help me get back the cows that were stolen from this ranch."

Deward spat again. "I'll fight them that killed Timoteo."

"It's one and the same bunch, Jake. You know that. Rustlers and murderers."

"A man risks his neck to get even for a friend that you had to bury. But it sorta galls a man to maybe cut his life off short by fightin' for Yankees."

"You've got a job, Jake. A lot of boys these days have nothing."

"All the same a man dies to avenge a friend and there's some reason to it. But die to save Yankee cows—" Deward shook his head. "All the boys feel the same way about it."

Con, feeling his weariness clear to his heels, checked a rising temper. He didn't want to say anything to further widen the breach between himself and his men.

He ate a silent meal with Coralee, told her she could have her pick of the bedrooms. He went down to the bunkhouse. Tonight there was no card game, no horseplay. The men rolled up in their blankets early. Con felt as if they almost resented his presence. A guard had been posted and their guns were at hand in the bunkhouse. But Con knew if there was trouble his crew would have no stomach for a fight.

Only Charlie Baston could he count on, now that Timoteo was dead. But Baston had a bad wound, and he was half-drunk. After the burial of Timoteo, Con had made him return to town. And stay at Doc Maxfield's this time until Doc said he was out of danger.

Shortly before dawn, Con awakened. He shook Sam Trench and told him to be sure and see that Coralee had something to eat. And also make sure she didn't leave Jawbone. He felt responsible for her safety. And he couldn't afford to let her go riding off somewhere, not with the range ready to blow up at any moment.

Saddling a blaze-faced roan, he rode out into the darkness. An hour past daylight he was deep in the Chisos, trying to visualize where the rustlers would be likely to strike next.

It was about the same as trying to predict where you'd see the next fur-legged tarantula climbing out of a wheel rut. It could be around the next hill. It could be forty miles south of the river. There was no doubt that even if his men were willing, it would be next to impossible to police the Jawbone range with a crew the size of his present one. And how much stomach did he have for this job? The question was glaring in his mind for only an instant and then he resolutely pushed it aside. Goddam it, he told himself, a man had to believe in something. He had to know what was right and do it. There was no putting aside what Grant and Lee had settled at Appomattox; you couldn't conveniently bathe your conscience in declaration that anything was ethical because the war had not ended as the North had been led to believe.

He wondered then as the sun beat down on his hat, with its patterns of sweat, just how much blame he could attach to himself for Timoteo's death. Had he accepted Arch's proposition would the Mexican now be alive?

It was about like saying that if it had rained another day last winter the grass would be that much greener this spring. He knew one thing for certain on this warm spring day, whether Yankee cows were stolen or not, whether Jawbone survived or fell, he would personally avenge Timoteo. This thing he would do, and if Arch died in the conflagration there was nothing that could be done about it.

On every hand, as he rode deeper into the Chisos, he saw familiar landmarks that brought back his youth. Hunting in these mountains with Arch. Setting out traps for the lobo wolf with Timoteo. Bringing along Rex, the dog Con had as a boy. Wherever Rex found occasion to pause by a bush, there a trap would be staked out. Because, Timoteo had explained, the lobo would not be able to resist the urge to mask a previous male odor with one of his own.

Everywhere he looked, the past came screaming back. He thought of his father and his brother. It was always Big Ed who rode with Poppa. And it wasn't until later that Con realized Poppa favored his first son because he looked like a Jason, while Con favored the Carters of Kentucky, his mother's people.

He thought of the day he traded a horse for a set of books owned by a frightened Abolitionist traveling by wagon to California. It was weeks before Poppa found the books and threw them into the fireplace.

"Don't blame Poppa," Big Ed said later. "He don't hate you, but you got to understand. He's been huntin' them books. He knowed you got 'em from that slave-lover. They found him hangin' to a tree west of here. And he'd been ridin' a Jawbone hoss. You know how Poppa feels about messin' with other folks' business. If men wants slaves, let 'em. This fella stirred up a passel of trouble down in Louisiana. And they chased him clean over here."

"My God, Ed," Con had cried. "That was *my* horse. I traded him for books. My books. And he was hanged. Is it a sin against the Almighty for a man to seek freedom for his black brothers?"

"Don't you never let Poppa hear you talk like that. You

just got to understand that God made a man black so's you know he's a slave—"

"Like God made Mexican women dark so you'd know it's all right to chase them into the brush and pin them to the ground?"

Big Ed flushed. "Well, me an' Arch don't do that no more. That Bible shouter that come to Santa Margarita put the fear in us with his hellfire talk."

"The fear was put in you," Con told his brother, "when you and some of your hooting friends paid a bottle of whisky to get a look at Ad Semple's belly razored off flat as a woman's."

And now riding into the Chisos today Con felt as helpless in his rage as he had the day he watched his father throw armload after armload of precious books into a roaring fire. Watching flames curl leather bindings, while Big Ed held his arms pinned to his sides.

And when it was done Poppa saying, "Let him go, Ed. Con, this should teach you to mind your own business. A man wants slaves or he doesn't want them is his business. Nobody else's, understand?"

"You proved it, Poppa. You burned my books."

"Sass won't buy you anything in this world but a broken head. You leave reading to folks who have nothing else to do. A Texas cowman has no time for burning his eyes out on fine print."

"You went to school," Con reminded. "Why not me?"

"Things were different in those days." The old man's face had turned bleak. "But I didn't have schooling enough, it seems. Not according to your mother's people."

It was years before Con managed even a partial forgiveness of his father for the episode of the books.

From a promontory he let his roan blow and scanned the uncounted miles of the Bend. Nothing moved. No dust trailing against the clear sky. No sound save his own breathing. The whicker of his horse. He saw his roan's ears shoot forward.

Jerking free his rifle from the boot, Con swung down and slipped noiselessly into a stand of juniper.

And he heard a man's voice, thinned by distance, say, "I tell you it was a hoss I heard. Up yonder on the ridge there."

Con wasn't sure but he thought it sounded like Leacham, the last of the old-time hands left on 88. Another man said, "You're spooked, old man. Wasn't nothin'."

"I don't like this worth a damn. Thievin' in broad daylight."

"Go back to the river, Leacham," the other man said in disgust. "And let Arch hold your hand."

Con felt a dryness in his throat. So it was Leacham after all. During the roundup just completed Jawbone and 88 had run a camp together. And Leacham had pitched in to help Sam Trench with the cooking.

Con moved forward until he came to the edge of a lip, and down through the screen of aspens that grew crookedly on a steep bank he could see Leacham, the sun cutting hat brim shadow on the prematurely aged face. And with Leacham was a tall man with an Adam's apple that jutted prominently under the sparse fringe of a blond beard. He had a rifle on the ground and was hunkered down, rolling a cigarette. A wide gun belt cinched in the lower portion of a sweat-marked wool shirt.

Their horses were not in sight, evidently tied off behind a shoulder of rock. From the looks of the two men they had been riding hard and had paused for a smoke. The evidence of their work was plain to see. Some fifteen head of Jawbone beef was bunched in a draw a short distance away.

Con brought back his rifle hammer. "Roundup's over, Leacham," Con said coldly. "Or hadn't you heard?"

The two men had seen him; saw the shine of sunlight on the long barrel of the rifle. Saw the tight brown face of the man behind it.

The blond-bearded man got slowly to his feet, his cigarette screwed up in a corner of his mouth as if it held a cigar.

"Got anything to say, Leacham?" Con snapped.

Leacham spread his hands. "I just do what I'm told."

"I can understand loyalty," Con said. "But when a man's boss turns thief it's time to look for a new job. Unless the man's a thief himself. Then it doesn't matter. Not unless he gets caught."

Leacham's face reddened. "I ain't no thief, Con."

Con nodded at the cows up the brushy draw. "Cattle

don't bunch themselves. They're driven. Looks mighty like thieving to me."

"Maybe I don't like it much," Leacham said carefully, watching the rifle in Con's hands. "But Arch is busted. What's a man to do these days?"

"He could fight for his ranch," Con said.

"You never fought for yours," Leacham said, and the blond-bearded man gave a short laugh. It quickly died when Con flicked him with his hard gaze. Leacham went on, "You just let them Yankees move onto Jawbone without even a holler from you."

"I no longer owned Jawbone. It was a legal sale."

"We figure we ain't stealin' from you, Con," Leacham said. "Takin' these cows that belong to Yankees, is just as legal as them takin' good land your poppa settled on years back."

"There's a difference. Any more of your bunch close by? Not that I'd expect an honest answer from you."

Leacham looked hurt. "Goddam it, Con, you had a chance to get a little of this money yourself and—"

"That's enough! In my father's time I'd take a rope and hunt for the nearest tree when I came on rustlers."

"You better get shut of talk like that right now," the blond-bearded man warned.

"Shut up, Traxton," Leacham said from the corner of his mouth. "Con don't have the stomach to hang a man."

"It's coming on me though, Leacham," Con said. "It's coming on me awful fast." He could feel pressure lines deepen at the corners of his mouth. "It's no longer just a case of rustling, Leacham. Timoteo's dead."

Leacham nodded. "I know. I'm damn sorry about that."

"Being damn sorry is going to give a man back his life?"

"I never killed him. Neither did Arch."

"You pen up a rattlesnake and if a hundred men are responsible for keeping the gate locked, they share the responsibility. If he gets loose, say, and bites some kid."

"Oh, hell, Con, that ain't the same."

"You're not working these cows alone," Con said. "I asked you once. Where's the closest bunch? I won't ask again."

"Five miles east," Traxton said, nodding over his shoulder.

"You work for Arch?" Con asked Traxton.

"I work for a fella in Mexico who's goin' to pay in gold for one helluva lot of beef."

Con knew he was one of the hardcases he had seen recently along the river, occupying the old rustler hangout at Vega Verde. "I don't think either one of you will collect any of that Mexican gold."

"What you aim to do with us, Con?" Leacham said, looking worried.

"I'm taking you to San Pablo. I want to see Sheriff Keeler get his lard out of a chair and lock you up for rustling. I'm going to make an example out of you two."

"You'll be blowin' a bugle in hell before you ever do that," Traxton said cockily.

"If I am," Con said, "you'll be right beside me helping me save up breath for the next blow. Now I want to see those gun belts drop. Easy."

"Con, wait a minute," Leacham protested. "I happen to know your own Jawbone boys don't give a damn whether these Yankee cows is stole or not—"

"I give a damn. Drop those belts. It's a long ride to San Pablo. You can go with whole hide or leaking your own blood. It's up to you."

"Mark me, Con," Leacham said, "one mornin' you'll wake up with a Yankee knife in your back. Sure as there's a nail in a coffin."

"Be sure it isn't your coffin with the nail in it. Now do what I told you. Now!"

Reluctantly the two men moved hands around to their belt buckles. The cattle up the draw were restive, trying to break out of the tight pack they were in and drift to good grass.

And in that moment, with sweat stinging the corners of his eyes, he heard the hoofbeats. Heard his horse in the aspens above catch the scent of approaching riders. Also heard the neighs of greeting from the horses of Traxton and Leacham tied off behind the shoulder of rock.

A brief hope flashed in Traxton's eyes. Leacham's face turned a dirty gray and for some reason Con was reminded of the haunted look the tragic Ad Semple used to get. As if he welcomed a means of escape from this predicament and at the same time dreaded the possible consequences.

Traxton was the first to make his play, as Con knew he would be, shouting, "Help! Jason's got us!"

But before Con could squeeze off a shot Traxton ducked behind Leacham. And Con knew in that instant that his reluctance to send a bullet crashing into Leacham could mean his own doom. Leacham, his face a pasty white jumped as Traxton fired over his shoulder. The bullet made a screaming green cut across the trunk of an aspen above Con's head.

There was shouting from beyond the shoulder of hill. A sharp acceleration of the hoofbeats. Somebody yelled, "Hang on, we're comin'!"

And Leacham, as if caught up in some nightmare tunnel made a desperate grab for his gun. It came up, spitting into the ground at Con's feet, spraying dirt on the front of his canvas pants. Dropping back, Con made a snap shot at Traxton's sweating face above Leacham's shoulder. But Leacham moved just then and the bullet struck his throat with such force that his head swung around sharply. His hat fell off as he caved in. Before he struck the ground there was a flashing arc of scarlet from his throat.

Without cover now, Traxton tried to reach the shelter of a deadfall, his gun slamming an erratic pattern of lead in Con's general vicinity. Con fired. A boot heel disintegrated. Traxton went flying just as seven riders swept around the shoulder of hill.

But Con was scrambling deeper into the trees. They had seen him up on the slope and with a wild Rebel yelling sent their horses up the grade after him. Traxton was waving them on. The only thing that saved him was the fact that they fired from the backs of running horses. Their aim was poor, but even so Con felt the slight tug of his hat band as a bullet whipped through the brim. If they caught him he'd die. By a bullet, if they were in a hurry. By a rope if they had time enough to enjoy it.

The leader was a big man with a scar that ran from eyebrow to jaw down the left side of his face. Wind whipped a red-and-white-checked shirt to his sweating torso. Behind him came six more riders on lunging horses. Halting his upward retreat, Con sent a bullet crashing at the center of the checkered shirt. The man sagged back, grabbed the horn. The next shot sent his horse rearing. It fell back on the rider directly behind. Two more horses fell. There was cursing, a scattering of shots. But Con had reached his own mount. He sent the roan streaking west. But they were after him. However, he knew this country better than most. He lured them on in a great circle and when they found themselves at the dead end of a box canyon, he was on a ledge, heading for higher ground. A chorus of frustrated yells and firing reached him. The bullets whipped harmlessly overhead.

When finally he reached Jawbone headquarters, the sickness in him had spread. His men were grouped by the bunkhouse door, watching him swing down from the lathered horse.

Jake Deward was the first to see the bullet hole in the brim of his hat: "Trouble?" the one-eyed man said.

"Of a sort. Leacham's dead. If you'd been with me, maybe I wouldn't have had to kill him."

The men exchanged glances and hung their heads. But none of them said they were sorry they hadn't been along to jump the rustlers of Yankee cows. And he supposed that they condemned him for Leacham's death. Not that he didn't have a right to defend his life. But because the die was cast and Jawbone cows were going to be rustled and Con, in trying to save Yankee dollars for Yankee pockets, had no business mixing in it and getting a good Texan killed.

He said, "If it's not asking too much, will one of you boys unsaddle my horse?" Deliberately he turned his back.

He went up to the house. Coralee, her pale hair in two thick plaits down her back, met him at the door.

"Nelda was here this afternoon," she said, her blue eyes wide.

"I'm surprised," he said tiredly and sank to a chair beside the big spur-scarred table. "What did she want?"

"To make up with you, I gathered." Coralee wiped the palms of her thighs along the narrow-legged britches. "I didn't know you'd quarreled."

"It's a little deeper than a quarrel."

Coralee's small white teeth bit into her lower lip. "She didn't like my being here."

"Nelda will have to learn that you can't cut grass and expect it to grow tall all in the same day."

"Before she left she said some ugly things." She sank to a

chair across the table from him and picked up his hat, which he had thrown on the dirt floor. She put a forefinger through the bullet hole in his hat. "Did you have this before you left this morning?"

"No. I had to kill one of Arch's men today. I feel as if the world had dropped out from under me. I've seen Leacham sitting at this table many times, playing cards with my father."

"I hope you don't have to kill Arch."

"A man should have no appetite after a day like this. But I have."

"I'll cook for you, if you like. It's a small way I can repay your kindness for letting me stay here."

His face relaxed sufficiently to give her a small smile. And he felt that a strong light had briefly touched his own dark world.

Chapter Sixteen

THAT AFTERNOON ARCH came into the camp at Vega Verde with sixty Jawbone cows pushed by twelve men. He had just helped himself to a tin of coffee from the pot on the sheet-iron stove when Jud Kilhaven said, "Hake's comin'." Kilhaven seemed almighty amused about something.

Arch Linnbrook turned and saw the lone rider fording the green waters of the Rio on a big bay horse. As Hake came out of the river, horse and man dripping, Arch could see the ugliness in the man's eyes, the paleness of the handsome mouth.

Hake swung down and slapped water off the brim of his hat. "Come here, Arch," he ordered, and walked down through the willows. Fuming at the peremptory command, Arch trailed along.

Hake halted at a sandy clearing and said, "Been hunting you for two hours."

"I just got in. What's up?"

"Con Jason jumped some of our boys. Leacham is dead. Traxton has a numb leg but was lucky to lose only a boot heel instead of a foot."

"Leacham—dead?" Arch swallowed and looked toward the rim that rose a thousand feet beyond the river. "My God only last month me an' Leacham went huntin' for bear up there."

"You poor simple fool," Hake said.

"I don't cotton to talk like that."

"Oh, you don't." Hake stood with hands on his hips, his black suit spotted with river spray. "Remember back in Missouri when you woke up from a drunk?"

"I ain't forgot."

"Well, you were drugged. Millie—a girl I knew—put something in your drink."

A cold fire began to build in Arch Linnbrook's gray eyes. "You're either loco or fired up on mescal to tell me a thing like that."

"I'm neither one. I'm just tired of trying to pump sense into your empty head. Maybe you didn't know it but Homer Peale was a great one for matching a man's handwriting. I'm sorry he's dead."

"You mean my signature on that bill-of-sale for the pool herd wasn't mine? Peale done it?"

Hake, a hard smile on his lips, nodded. "You sold out your neighbors, Arch. You know what they'd do to you if they found out for sure?"

"They wouldn't do one damn thing," Arch said stoutly, but his voice wavered a little at the end.

"They may be afraid of you. But if they had definite proof," Hake went on coldly, "they'd catch you some dark night."

"This definite proof you talk about," Arch said, his voice deadly, "wouldn't mean much if there was nobody left alive to tell about it."

Hake ignored this. "And to think I once believed you showed promise. Arch, you're a weakling."

"Who the hell you callin' weak?"

"You can't even follow orders. I wrote you to make Con Jason the one proposition. If he didn't show interest you were to forget it. But you persisted. And I imagine you got your sister to help in the inducement."

"In about one second you're goin' to be starin' up at the Mex sky and not seein' one damn thing."

"I don't mind a grasping, greeding woman. As long as there is a certain passion with her greed."

Arch's face turned a choking red. He made a pass at his belt but Bentley Hake said, "Jud."

And from behind him Arch heard Jud Kilhaven's voice: "You want it, Arch, you'll get it. Right in the back!"

Arch stood rigid, his right hand out from his gun butt. And at last he lowered his hand and licked his lips.

Hake said, "That's better. You should tell your sister not to show her eagerness to get married again."

"*Again!* She ain't never been married."

"Tell him, Jud."

"I run into a fella over by Joplin," Jud Kilhaven said over Arch's shoulder. "He told me about a weddin' in St. Louis. Your sister, Arch."

"I don't believe it. Why wouldn't she tell me?"

"Probably she knows your weaknesses as well as I do," Bentley Hake said. "She couldn't trust you to keep her secret. When the war that she was so sure would last for twenty years was suddenly concluded, she hurried to Texas to pick up her life again. She was a little too eager with Con Jason, I guess. As she was with me. Second best, I was. A position I don't enjoy in the affections of a woman."

Arch started for him, big fists clenched, but Jud Kilhaven's gun rammed sharply into his spine. Arch halted.

Hake said, "Because we've been associates, after a fashion. And because I do owe something to your sister, I'm willing to offer a slight payment."

"Payment for what?" Arch demanded.

"The favors of Nelda. Pay for every damn head of beef you have on your range."

"Steal my beef? You'll have to walk over my dead body!"

"One thing for sure," Hake said coolly, "it would be cheaper that way. But I'll pay five hundred dollars. As I did last year in Missouri. I'll send you a draft from Chihuahua City. And when you get it, consider yourself the luckiest man who ever drew breath."

"The day I met you my luck was hid behind a black star."

"Don't haggle with me. I'll be tempted to reduce my generous offer." Hake laughed.

Arch turned on his heel, brushed past Jud Kilhaven, who

held a cocked revolver. He swung into the saddle and looked at his men from 88.

"All right boys, let's pull out."

They just looked at him. Then they swung their eyes to Hake, who had come up to lean against a willow.

"One thing you didn't learn, Arch," he said. "When you turn thief you have to go all the way. You can't have moments of regret. You sold these boys a bright story of riches in Mexico. They believe in it. You, unfortunately, are stupid enough to let old friendships cut the bridge out from under you. I'm referring to Con Jason."

Arch showed his teeth, seemed about to speak, then broke off.

Hake said, "You fired your old crew in Missouri last year. I suppose you know it was a mistake."

"Everything since I met you has been a mistake."

"The only man who might have sided you in this was Leacham. But he's dead. Get out of here, Arch, and don't come back."

Arch Linnbrook rode out, his horse splashing into the river. Jud Kilhaven lifted his rifle, sighting it on the broad back. Hake shook his head.

"He'll be dead soon enough anyway. I owe him a little unpleasantness. To repay his sister. In her anger she flaunted the talents of another man in my face. It was a mistake on her part." This last he said under his breath and turned and walked over to the monte game being played on a blanket in the shade of the willows.

He felt apart from these men. Apart from everyone else in the world, even his brother who had joined up with Quantrill and taken the name of Kilhaven, their mother's name.

Hake wondered then when the change had taken place in him. At first it had been the war and the fight for survival. And then it had just gone on and on into other things and there seemed to be no stopping.

When he had been taken prisoner he learned many things. He knew the conflict couldn't last, because he was held in Yankee territory and he could see the vast preparations for the final onslaught aimed to crush the South. He didn't believe the wild rumors so prevalent at the time in places such as St. Louis; the war would go grindingly on for two more decades at least. People like Nelda Linnbrook had believed this. She had decided to grab a little of life when she could. But she had become widowed—

As a prisoner, Hake had begun to build for the future. His connections had started to bear fruit. Like the Chicago incident. He knew he was liked by those rich men and they had made him a partner in Alliance because he convinced them he knew the cattle business. But then he had taken seven thousand dollars and lost it on a gamble for quick profits.

In this moment Hake wondered if his ability for pulling wires to make people jump would one day be the death of him. It was an unsettling thought. But if all went well he would be very much alive. And with sufficient means to live as a gentleman. Even if he would be forced to live out his life in Mexico.

This thinking here on the edge of the Rio with the Mexican sun burning across his shoulders was not good. The only saving of a man's sanity lay in action. This much he had learned in the war. You sit around and think and the awesome prospect of your doom becomes too great a burden to carry. And to retain your sanity you turn to violence.

You dig a stick into a pool and soon you discolor the water—

His brother Jud came up, rifle under a long thin arm. "You figure to give Arch five hundred for his cows?"

Hake gave his brother a cold smile. "You ought to know better than that."

"Well, I just wondered if this Mex heat was gettin' to your brain."

"Don't let it get to yours, Jud."

"You got a reason for sayin' that?"

"Last night you mentioned Coralee Whitley in your sleep."

"You had your chances with her," Jud Kilhaven said.

"I don't care for women who've had money. And then lost it." Hake tapped his brother on the chest. "Charley Quantrill is dead. Remember that the kind of war he fought against men—and women—is also dead."

"How about the business you had with Arch's sister."

"I suspect you also had a little business there, Jud. That sort of thing is different. She was willing. On both occasions she was willing. At least she wasn't marked up, so I imagine your association with her was like mine."

"This Coralee Whitley—"

"You stay away from her. We've got a chance to grab ourselves a nice chunk of Mexican gold. We've got the boys here in the Bend on our side, because we're fighting that Yankee cattle company. But they'd hang you sure as sunrise if you use your Quantrill tricks against a girl like Coralee."

Jud Kilhaven said, "Don't hurt a man to talk about it. In his sleep." Kilhaven added, "How long before we finish up this job?"

"You're the cattle expert. How long does it take to drive eight or nine thousand head of beef to Chihuahua?"

Traxton had come up. He wore a new pair of boots. "Con Jason will follow us. He'll get some men somewhere."

"Won't make much difference if he recruits a small army," Bentley Hake said. "My Mexican friend from Chihuahua has vaqueros. Lots of them. It could be an interesting battle."

"Maybe this damn Mex friend of yours will put a knife at our throats once he gets his hands on them cows."

Hake shrugged. "He may try. If he does he won't be the first man to have the top of his skull laid open like a ruptured melon."

Jud Kilhaven said, "How long you figure it'll take them boys in Chicago to start on your trail?"

"If any one of them comes it'll be Leroy Marcom. He's the only one who can sit a horse decently or shoot a gun." Hake smiled. "You can imagine the sort of reception an ex-Yankee major will get in these parts."

"But you said he'd been here before," Traxton put in. "When Alliance took Jawbone over. They never run him out then."

"He was a businessman then, spending Yankee money in Santa Margarita. When he comes this time he'll be pitted against Bentley Hake, late of the CSA. The picture will be entirely different. However, I hope we'll be through with our business here. If and when he comes."

"If he tries to hire men," Kilhaven said, "I reckon he won't have no more luck than Con Jason."

"I imagine not," Hake said, and told one of the men to

saddle him a fresh horse. "Marcom is a Yankee. Jason is known as a Yankee-lover. It adds up to the same thing."

Chapter Seventeen

THAT NIGHT, AFTER three hour's sleep in the bunkhouse, Con decided to ride to town. He went up to the house. It was still early evening. Coralee sat at the big table. Lamp glow touched the room. Con did something he had forgotten to take care of before.

He gave her a small revolver. "In case there's trouble," he said.

"Arch is your enemy," she said, her pale-blue eyes watching his face.

"It was his choice, not mine. Blow out the lamp when I leave." And he wondered just where she would be safer, here or at the hotel in town. But could Arch be trusted in his present reckless mood? He knew Arch's murderous rages all too well. Arch would be hard to hold now that Coralee had turned him down.

He wanted to explain how he felt but his mind was still fogged from the nap in the bunkhouse. "You stay put here," he told her. "We'll work this thing out."

"I should get out. It won't do my reputation any good to continue staying here."

"Just do as I ask," he said, more brusquely than he intended. "If something happened to you in town—well, you'd be on my conscience."

"Don't let that trouble you." She got up from the table. "I came from town alone. I can return the same way. I wouldn't want to burden your conscience."

"I didn't mean it quite that way. But you're not leaving here tonight. So forget it."

"Then you intend holding me against my will?"

"You came here asking for help—"

"Only because you offered it."

"I do intend to help you." He tried to smile. "But there are other things that have to be done first."

She looked at him while insects beat their senseless heads against the lamp chimney. "I'm sorry that I've only added to your troubles," she sighed. "I know from what I overheard in town that things haven't been going easy for you."

He had been staring out into the yard, where a rectangular smear of yellow poured from the bunkhouse doorway. "Maybe you're the only good thing that has happened to me in a long time."

He went out, closing the door behind him. He wondered then just why a bit of light comes into a man's life when there is so much darkness. He wondered just how much of a fool he was to make this fight for Jawbone. Running a ranch for absentee owners was a far cry from running it yourself, Con had learned. The endless reports. Working with a skeleton crew. Then the coming of Kilhaven and Peale. And the rest of it.

Obviously Bentley Hake was swindling his Chicago partners and he knew he should probably be pleased that men who knew nothing of the cattle business—Northerners at that— were being slicked out of their money. But in him was a hard core of the things he had read in the books loaned by Doc Maxfield through the years. Or maybe it came from his mother's people. He was named for his uncle, Doc Maxfield said. He wondered about this uncle he had never seen. He wondered just how much decency, integrity, is passed from one generation to another. Or is it all acquired during a man's brief span of life. Or not acquired at all, as in the case of Bentley Hake.

And although he hated Arch Linnbrook for the way things had turned out, he couldn't help but recognize a certain validity to the man's argument to turn thief. After all, as Arch had said once when this business of rustling had first come up, what Texas cowman hadn't stolen beef? Con had heard his own father brag many times that anything on four legs caught within what he considered to be the rightful boundaries of Jawbone immediately became his property. The boundaries of Jawbone extended some miles beyond what a court of law would recognize. But this didn't deter the old man. And Bert Linnbrook had also done his share of casting with a wide loop to get his start here in the Bend. And Bert

Linnbrook had passed this philosophy of grab and hang on, no matter how, to his son, Arch.

He was nearly to the bunkhouse when Charlie Baston staggered out and weaved down to the nearest corral. Sight of his *segundo* sparked the building pressures in Con. He said, "Charlie, goddam it, I told you to get to town!"

Baston wheeled, nearly lost his balance, then righted himself. The pack of white bandage at right shoulder and arm was filthy. "I been waitin' for you to do somethin' about Timoteo," Baston said, his voice thick from the whisky he had consumed. "You ain't moved off your tail. So I'll go do it myself."

With an oath Con came up, caught Baston by his good arm. This tough man who had come here with his father so long ago. The last of the old ones left, now that Timoteo was gone. Something tightened in him when he thought of the old Mexican and how he had died.

"Charlie, listen to me. I'll get the man responsible for Timoteo's getting killed. But you get to town like I told you. Do what Doc Maxfield tells you—"

"You need me. You need a fightin' man. Even a one-armed fightin' man."

"If you're trying to commit suicide," Con said, exasperated, "why don't you put a gun muzzle in your mouth like Mark Dollop did?"

"I aim to kill Jud Kilhaven. It was his hoss that was found near Timoteo. Ad Semple never killed the Mex. Cut him, maybe, but never killed him."

"If you were so sure, why didn't you stop the hanging? You were there."

" 'Cause he deserved to get his goddam neck busted. For cuttin' on a man. Even a dead man."

"Charlie, do what I told you. Doc is—"

"I aim to help you." The big, grizzled man weaved again on rubbery legs.

"In your condition you couldn't shoot the jackrabbit you held by the ears at arm's length."

"You aim to go after Kilhaven?" Charlie Baston said from a corner of his mouth. "Or do you aim to stand here all night talkin' about it?"

"Get back to town. Ride with me." Con was losing his

patience. "Goddam it, why do you hang another weight around my neck?"

"Ain't no weight around your neck, sonny. You're just yellow clear down to your boot heels."

"Nobody else could get away with saying that!"

"You jabber like an' old woman, but you don't do nothin'. If your poppa or Big Ed was alive they'd have Kilhaven hangin' by now."

"If you don't want to work for me any longer, by God you can quit!"

Charlie Baston took a long drink from a bottle he dragged up from a hip pocket. The men, gathered around the bunkhouse door, were silently watching.

Baston said, "If you had any guts you'd tell them Yankees in Chicago to fight for their own damn cows. You'd take your own herd and you'd grab that Nelda woman by the hair of her head and go off somewheres an' make your own life."

Con bit back a retort. He thought of Charlie Baston in the old days, teaching him to ride, to shoot a gun. Poppa was always too busy with Big Ed to be bothered. Con said, his voice softer, "Charlie, I know how you feel about the Yankees. But things aren't quite as simple as you claim. I just can't walk out on my obligations."

"The only obligation you got is to kill Jud Kilhaven."

"That I'll do. If it takes me ten years."

"Let's you an' me go find him."

"Charlie, use your head." Con pointed out that Hake's force outnumbered theirs at least three to one. "And there's no telling how many more he can get across the river."

"Then what do you aim to do?" Charlie Baston leered. "Stand here an' die of old age?"

"My father threw his life away on just such a foolhardy venture. And he sacrificed my brother along with himself. The thousand head of beef Hake ran off was easy because the cows were bunched. But the rest of the Jawbone cows are scattered from here to hellangone. It'll take time and they'll have to spread themselves thin." He projected his voice, looking toward the men by the bunkhouse. "I'm hoping you all will help me. It's when we'll get Kilhaven."

With an oath Charlie Baston got his horse and rode away

into the darkness. Con didn't even try and stop him. What was the use?

Con came up to the bunkhouse where Deward lounged in the doorway. The other men had gone inside. Over east the moon was beginning its ascent.

"Hake has the superior force, Jake. But we can hit him and run. Are you with me?"

"Lee tried that. It didn't work out for him." Deward thoughtfully rubbed his eyepatch. "I'm in favor of clearin' out after we get Kilhaven. We got nothin' here no more, Con."

Con started to say something about loyalty. Then changed his mind. He said he was going to town to build a fire under Barney Slager. "I'm hoping he's sent word to the sheriff. If he hasn't one of you boys will have to go."

"Takin' the gal with you?"

"She's safer here. If it was daylight it might be different. No telling what a man can run into in the dark. Jake, I don't have to remind you that she's a lady."

"You don't. I'll keep an eye on her."

"Thanks, Jake. Take first guard trick. If I'm not back by midnight have Dave take over."

Con rode out, the moon at his back. Somehow this land seemed alien to him now. He had made the fight to try and keep a small part of Jawbone in Jason hands—as his father would want. Even though the small part of Jawbone was a four-hundred-head herd of cattle. Even though he no longer owned Jawbone, he thought he could see that it was run properly, at least. With himself as manager. But it hadn't worked out.

As he headed for town, his gun loose in its holster, he thought of Coralee in the house where he had been born. He thought of her desire to see Tucson and build a new life for herself. And he began to wonder if maybe out in Arizona they had stopped fighting the war. And maybe a man could put his hand around a glass of whisky in some good saloon and have the talk be of cattle or weather or whatever. Instead of the inevitable talk of "what we'll do to them blue-bellies next time we fight," as was the case in most Texas bars these days.

He saw the lights of Santa Margarita in the distance. And

the sight brought him no pleasure, even though it had in the past. How glad he had been to get back here after the war. But now he felt like a stranger.

Chapter Eighteen

WHEN CON RODE in he saw Harvey Pearce step out of the livery stable down the block and hurry toward him. The fat night hostler was out of breath when he came up. "Nelda Linnbrook said if you come to the stable I was to give you a message," Pearce wheezed.

"I'm not much interested, Harvey, but thanks just the same."

"You better see her. She's some hotted up about somethin'." Pearce jerked a hand at the hotel across the street. "She's stayin' over there till things quiet down around here. Lucky I seen you ride in—"

Nelda's voice called from the hotel door. "Con! I want to see you!"

With a weary sigh Con crossed over. She had come to the walk, and in the lamplight spilling from the hotel, he could see the fury in her green eyes. "Just what do you think you're doing!" Nelda demanded.

"Not much of anything that people around here approve of. So it seems. What seems to be your complaint?"

"Coralee at your place. Do you really think I'll let you flaunt her right in my face?"

"I'm not flaunting, Nelda. But I don't care much whether you like it or not."

"That's a fine attitude for you to have. When we've been promised to each other for so long."

Con gave a slow shake of his head. A buggy rattled into town and wheeled through the stable doorway. "I've learned one thing. A promise doesn't mean much to a Linnbrook."

He saw her shoulders stiffen and then she sagged. "You mean because of my father selling you out."

"You know what I mean. Bentley Hake. I saw you together. It was pretty obvious."

"He's a friend of Arch's."

"And a friend of yours."

"I'm willing to give you another chance, Con. But you'll have to be reasonable. First, you must get Coralee out of town."

"I will, in my own good time."

She leaned forward, glaring at him. "Con, it wouldn't be very healthy for you if Arch knew Coralee was at your place."

"I imagine he'd think the worst. Knowing Arch."

"He loves that girl, but I can't see why." Nelda pushed a hand against the mass of dark-red hair. "She's a wanton. I could tell you things. Things that happened during the war."

"I wouldn't believe much of anything you said, Nelda."

"Her St. Louis home became quite a rendezvous for our CSA boys on leave. They found her comforting."

"That's a vile thing to say."

"But you're in doubt," she said, smiling with a faint triumph.

He turned his back and crossed over to Slager's.

"If Arch learns about you and Coralee, he'll kill you!" she screamed at him.

He looked back, but she had swept into the hotel.

When he entered Slager's the men at the bar and the gaming tables looked at him silently. Slager said, "Seems like I detected a little wildcat in Nelda's voice just then. Looks like you got a passel of troubles, Con. Includin' them caused by wimmen."

"I have other things on my mind." Putting his back to the bar, he addressed the men—some fifteen—gathered there, telling them he needed good riders. Men not afraid to fight.

"I thought we could join in a common cause," Con said without much hope, "as we have before in the Bend."

His plea was greeted by a stony silence. At last Billy Snider, who had been sitting with his feet against the wall and the front legs of the chair tipped off the floor, thumped down the legs and stood up. "Maybe I speak for these boys, Con, I dunno," the rancher said. In the lamplight his side whiskers looked like gray brush. "But I sure as hell speak for myself. You pa was my friend. If a Jason still owned Jawbone we'd be spillin' all over each other tryin' to help. But if them goddam blue-shirts in Chicago lose their beef, good riddance."

Barney Slager said, "Con, you got a few head of beef in your own name. Why don't you locate somewheres down in the Chisos. You ever need a hand then and we'll come runnin'."

"You boys talk a mighty good philosophy," Con said, his bitter eyes sweeping over the barroom. "But there isn't a man here who'd turn his back on Yankee money if he had the chance to get any."

"We'll take their money," Slager informed him, "but when it comes to fightin' for 'em—"

"Looks as if I'll have to send to Paso," Con interrupted, "if I want some good men. Or maybe clear to Mesilla."

This was greeted by a stiffening silence. Billy Snider came across the floor, grinding his teeth. "Let an old man give you a bit of advice, son. Don't bring no gunslingers into this country."

"They're already here. Jud Kilhaven. Bentley Hake and the crowd they're with."

"You'd be fightin' against one of our own," Snider went on stoutly. "Arch Linnbrook."

For a moment Con was too astonished to speak. Then he said, "You of all people, Billy. Sticking up for Arch."

"I know it don't seem reasonable," the old rancher said with a shake of his head. "I hate Arch's guts. 'Cause I know as well as I got boot heels on hard Texas floor that he sold me an' my friends down the river when he lost that pool herd. But even so, he's Texan. If Arch can help steal Yankee cows, then he's got my vote."

"I'll be good goddamned," Con said with disbelief.

"Oh, I'll settle with Arch in my own good time," Billy Snider went on narrowly. "But I don't aim to set still an' see Yankee money hire gunhands to kill him. To protect Yankee cows."

Con swallowed a sharp anger. "It's the uniform again. Just like the war. The hell with what the man may be like who wears it. Just so he wears gray he's on our side."

"That's the way the boot fits," Snider said.

"If he wears blue he can be a saint but we'll still try to kill him. Or wreck him financially."

"If we don't believe that," Slager said, "what else do we have to believe in."

"Why, you can believe in lots of things, Barney. You can let your passions run away with you, for one thing, and hang a poor simple fool like Ad Semple. And you can be righteous about it all at the same time."

"Well, we was a mite hasty, mebbe," Slager admitted, "but Semple wasn't no good to himself nor anybody else."

"You're setting a mighty tall saddle, Barney," Con snapped. "You're getting up almost as high as God almighty to decide a thing like that. Gentlemen," he said, his gaze coldly sweeping the room, "for the first time I'm ashamed of being a Texan."

"Won't buy you no friends talkin' like that," Slager warned, his face reddening.

"I'm beginning to wonder if I have any friends." With a shaking hand Con poured himself a drink. The whisky only intensified his frustration. "I don't suppose I have to ask," he said, turning to Slager, "whether or not you sent a man to tell the sheriff I may need help."

Slager met his gaze. "After you left here I asked the boys about it. They don't want no Texas sheriff savin' dollars for that bunch in Chicago. I got to admit, I agree."

"I see." Con slammed his empty glass on the bar and started out.

"Con, don't do some fool thing," Billy Snider cut in, "that'll turn us against you for all time."

Con halted, looked around. "Can't you boys understand? If we don't have some law here we're doomed." He looked around the long room with its gaming tables, the faces of roughly clad men under their dirty hats. "The war is done," he went on, "and we have to live in a civilized world again."

"The war is done?" Billy Snider said. He spat on the floor. "I'd let Arch Linnbrook swindle me out of another hundred head of cows, if I could hear your pa shout from the grave how he feels about what you just said."

"He wouldn't agree, I admit—"

"I tell you what your pa and Big Ed would've done," Snider said, shaking a bony finger under Con's nose. "If Bert Linnbrook sold them out an' some Yankee boys come south to take over Jawbone—" Snider gave a harsh laugh. "Them Yankees would've had to take over at the point of a gun. There'd been dead Yankees out there at Jawbone."

"And ever' man in the Bend," Slager added, "would've been behind your pa and Big Ed."

"Your loyalties baffle me," Con said with a twist of his lips. "Bert Linnbrook betrayed a trust by selling me out. His son takes a pool herd north and loses it. And yet you stick up for Bert and his son. You despise men who invest in Texas cows and Texas land. Just because they're Nawth."

"We're all a little surprised you never fought for them Jawbone cows yourself, Con," Billy Snider snapped. "But now that Jawbone is owned by Yankees you get your back bowed. It's a little late, if you ask me."

The old man turned his back and shuffled to a dark corner where he sat down in his favorite chair and tipped it back against the wall.

"Can't you understand," Con went on patiently, "that Jawbone was legally sold? That if I killed the men trying to dispossess me it would have been murder?"

"You mean you never killed a Yankee?" Slager said.

"I killed a man in uniform. I killed him to keep from being killed. But that was war."

"And we been tryin' to tell you the war ain't over. It never will be."

Doc Maxfield, smoking his pipe, had entered quietly. Now he said, "Con's right. You boys are wrong."

Billy Snider slammed down the legs of his chair. "By God, Doc, if there was another doctor within ninety miles of here you wouldn't say that."

"But there *isn't* another doctor." Smiling faintly, Doc Maxfield looked up at Con. "I told you once I enjoyed a certain immunity here."

There was a sudden faint rumble in the distance that sounded like thunder. But the sound was too constant for that, Con decided. Tilting his head, Con listened, his mind swinging sharply back to sounds of the war. Cavalry. Every man was on his feet. Con stepped outside and peered down the moon-swept street.

In a few moments a large body of riders came swinging down the stage road from the north. Hand on his gun, Con tensely watched them approach. And in the pool of light spilling from the saloon, with men crowded around to look at these riders, a brown-suited man on a white horse said crisply, "Hello, Jason. You remember me. I'm Leroy Marcom."

Con said nothing. Marcom swung down. He did not offer to shake hands. He looked around at the men peering over the doors, packed at the windows of Slager's. Marcom was a tall man. He wore a revolver and his boots were caked with mud.

There were about twenty men with Marcom.

Marcom waved a hand at a stocky man who had come up, a sawed-off shotgun under his arm. "Jason, this is Allan Smoot. He was my sergeant. And these are my men. I hired them in Kansas."

"You're just in time," Con said, 'if you want to save Jawbone."

"I hope so," Marcom said stiffly; his mustache curved thinly down over an equally thin mouth.

And over the swing doors Billy Snider said, "The Yankee Army come to Texas, by God." Then he added, "You'll have a Yankee knife in your back yet, Con."

Chapter Nineteen

BECAUSE HE HAD been coming to this place since boyhood, Arch Linnbrook knew how best to approach the house without being seen. After first gauging the breeze on this spring night, he rode west and left his mount deep in the cottonwoods planted by Con's father years ago. When they were boys Arch and Con used to climb the spindly trunks. Now the trees towered into the night sky. A sturdy growth, symbolic of the ties between the Jason and the Linnbrook families. As Arch stared at the dark buildings of Jawbone ahead, he wondered just how he would explain to Con that he, Arch Linnbrook, had been wrong. Admitting a mistake did not come easy to a Linnbrook. As he cautiously approached the house, downwind from the corraled Jawbone horses, he thought of his father's last moments. Maybe because those last moments concerned the man he was going to see this night.

He remembered Bert Linnbrook in the big bed at 88 ranch house. Gaunt and in pain and not understanding the sudden unevenness of his pulse; the pain deepening along his left side and arm. An 88 rider had gone to summon Doc Maxfield. Nelda was bathing her father's forehead with a damp towel. The war was only a few months finished.

"Wonder what Rand Jason and Big Ed would say if they knowed I sold Con out?"

"Hush, Father," Nelda admonished. "Save your strength."

Bert Linnbrook's head turned on the pillow. "I tried to make a lady out of you," he said tiredly. "That Saint Looey school cost me enough, God knows."

"Maybe it would have been better," Nelda snapped, "if you'd never sent me there."

"You sayin' I wasted my money?"

"I might be satisfied with things as they are. But thanks to your money and that school, I'm not satisfied."

"You better be satisfied, 'cause you're goin' to marry Con and life won't be no picnic here in Texas for ten years, maybe—"

"Thanks to you," Nelda said, her green eyes bitter, "Con no longer owns Jawbone. He's only a hired hand."

Bert Linnbrook's mouth became as gray as the rest of the face that for some sixty-odd years had felt the lash of storm and blinding sun on this and other frontiers. "Maybe I done wrong," he admitted grudgingly, "but Rand made me so goddam mad, wantin' to borrow fightin' money from me. When ever' man with a feather-weight of brains knowed the war was lost to the South."

"Why don't you tell Con that?" Arch said. "He don't feel kindly toward you for peddlin' them notes."

"I don't have to explain to him. He's as iron-headed as his pa was. I tried to tell him the South couldn't win."

"Then why did you loan him money?" Nelda demanded. "To fight a war you didn't believe in?"

"Rand was such a know-it-all," Linnbrook said. "I wanted to have him up short and listen to him beller."

"Yankee cannon took care of his beller," Arch said.

"The poor old fool," Bert Linnbrook said. "He's likely got hell's front door propped open for me."

"You'll be all right," Arch said. "Once the doc gets here."

Bert Linnbrook gazed at the rain-marked ceiling. "Reckon I struck a blow for the Union by lettin' Rand Jason have that money so him and Big Ed could squander it on guns and hosses and men. And then get the whole thing chewed to pieces."

"One thing I have to be thankful for," Nelda said, her mouth white. "You kept your Union sympathies to yourself. It wouldn't have made my life easy around here if you hadn't."

"I ain't the only Texan that felt that way."

"Why didn't you hold it against Arch?" Nelda said. "He fought for the South." She glanced across the bed at her brother, maliciously. She blamed Arch for not coming out of the war with money enough to give her some of the basic comforts.

"Me and Arch had our words about the war," Bert Linnbrook said. "But once a boy gets bit by the war bug there's no holdin' him."

Nelda said, "How is the pain now, Father?"

"You know I feel one hell of a lot better. Now you clear out and let me talk to my boy. Somethin' I should have brung up before."

Nelda hesitated, biting her lip. Then, shrugging, she did as her father asked, quietly closing the door behind her.

"This is man-to-man talk, Arch." Bert Linnbrook struggled to a sitting position and Arch slipped a pillow behind his back. "You might as well know the truth, boy. I was some put out when you joined the Johnny Rebs."

"I know you was, Pa."

"Ain't no use airin' your peeves in front of wimmen folks. Even if Nelda is your sister. It's somethin' for you to remember, boy, when I'm gone."

"You'll be here for a long time, Pa."

"Yeah. A fist-full of minutes ago I figured I was a goner. But now— Well, you listen close. It might be a spell before I can set a saddle easy and you'll have to run things. And you might as well know the truth. But keep it from your sister, 'cause she'll fret and make you miserable carping about bad times."

Arch, his mouth dry, said, "You sayin' we're broke?"

"I made some bad investments in the war."

"You should've talked things over with me," Arch complained.

"You was off fightin' a war, remember?"

Arch colored. "You never yet treated me like a man."

"You're a damn kid. You never growed up. Brawlin' ever' time you get in a hot wind."

"I went to war 'cause I never figured to stay home and let you run me like a twenty-a-month cowhand."

"Don't use that voice on me, boy," the old man said sternly. "I made this ranch, you never. When I'm gone, if there's anything left, it's yours and Nelda's. But until then you mind your talk."

Arch's face was white, but he said nothing.

Bert Linnbrook went on, "I want Nelda to marry with Con. He's a hard worker. He knows the cow business—"

"I s'pose I don't know a cow from a Spanish tick."

"As Nelda's husband, Con will be able to take over here and put this place back on its feet. And you work with him, hear?"

"I never figured Con to be so damn smart. If he was, how come he stood still an' let you sell him out."

"It was an obligation his pa made. Con honored it. He believes in the law, in doin' things the right way. The way they should be done."

"And I s'pose," Arch sneered, "you always done things the right way." Arch gave a short laugh.

"No. And neither did Con's pa. But things is different than they was in the old days." The old man sank back on his pillows, staring again at the rain spots on the ceiling. "This end of Texas won't mean a damn till we get decent law. We need Con in this family."

"Like I need a jackass with five legs."

"And Nelda needs somebody to hold the reins tight," Bert Linnbrook went on, ignoring Arch. "I spoiled that gal. And without Con she won't be no good to any man."

"You talk like Con was St. Peter on a white hoss."

"Goddam it, you mind your talk—"

Arch bit back a retort, because one glance at the slack jaw and the eyes no longer interested in the intricate brown patterns of weather stains on the ceiling told him his father was dead.

And even though later he would try and deny it, he secretly blamed his outburst over Con for causing his father's death. And in a parceling out of the guilt feeling so heavy in him, he also blamed Con. With the passage of time he was able to modify his resentment of Con. But it was just under the surface. It particularly rankled when Con refused to throw in with him on Hake's plan to strip Jawbone of cattle, because it pointed up so clearly the things his father had said about Con.

But now Arch had to admit Con was right in not taking one of the hooks from Bentley Hake's throw lines, while he, Arch, had taken bait, hook, and swallowed a good deal of line. Like any stupid catfish in the Rio, where he and Con used to fish when they were boys. His blood was still stinging when he recalled how Hake brazenly admitted duping him of the pool herd in Missouri.

Now as Arch crept through the cottonwoods toward the Jawbone ranchhouse, he guessed maybe the old man's evaluation of him was right. He needed Con's steadying hand. He'd have a talk with Nelda and get her to see things in a new light. He'd never given her any details concerning that final talk with the old man, how Pa had wanted Con to take over at 88. Well, he needed Con now because they would have to stand together to fight off Hake.

And he would straighten up that business about Timoteo. He would tell Con that Kilhaven had killed him in a fight over a horse, which was God's truth. Con would understand. He'd have to. And Arch would let him know that there were no hard feelings about Leacham getting killed. It was going to be Con and Arch standing off Hake. And with Con then helping run 88 as it should be run.

Arch dreamed the big dream. As a result of Con making a success at 88, Nelda would have money. And Arch further vowed he would have Nelda straighten things up with Coralee Whitley.

He and Coralee and Con and Nelda. They could live together in the one house until another could be built at 88. And Con could throw in his own cows, those he had taken from Alliance in lieu of wages. Con was such a prideful man, he'd want to chuck something of his own into the pot.

A warm glow touched him and he felt a sudden great

affection for his boyhood friend. And when things settled
down, his thoughts continued on the bright pathway, their
kids, Coralee's and Nelda's, would go whooping across the
range.

Smiling into the moon-lanced grove, Arch had to admit
that much as he once had hated the idea, the old man was
right in his last wish to have Con become a part of 88. A full
partner, yessiree. They'd get to Paso and have a lawyer draw
up the papers. And maybe in a year or so they could each
take a honeymoon after they sold some beef. He'd let Con
and Nelda go first. Then he and Coralee would go clear to
San Francisco, maybe, if she wanted to.

Arch, living in a wide golden dream, jerked to a halt when
he saw a flare of light far down the yard. Someone touching
match to cigar or cigarette. So Con had set guards out. That
was good precaution, but once they combined forces at 88,
they'd have discipline with the men like in the war. No more
of this foolish business of a man acting as night picket giving
away his position with a match flare.

Hugging the deep shadows of the house wall, Arch crept
to the front door, which he knew was usually left unlocked.
And he found it this way. Grinning, he slipped into the
house. Con would be some surprised when he learned how
easily his old friend had gained access to the house. Jeb Stuart wasn't the only commander who taught his men to use
the night for cover.

Unerringly he made his way across the familiar parlor to
Con's bedroom. The grin still tight on his lips, he leaned over
the big bed and whispered, as he used to do in the old warm
days of youth, "Hey, boy. Time to go fishin'—"

He broke off as he found himself staring into wide frightened eyes in the pale oval of a face that was quartered by
moonlight streaming through a side window. The large "O"
of a frightened mouth. Still white fingers clutching an edge
of blanket to a slender pulsing throat. At the edge of each
clutching hand two thick plaits of hair lay across the blanket
like strands of rope made from hemp the color and texture
of cornsilk.

"Arch," she whispered, and recognition, but no lessening
of fear, was in her wide staring eyes.

Without a sound Arch swept both plaits of hair into one

large hand and jerked her upright in the bed. And as she desperately tried to cling to the blanket, he jerked it away from her upper body. Rage made a fist in his throat. Too frightened to make an outcry, she sat numbly while he continued to hold her braided hair. His angry eyes flashed over her white length where moonlight made the flesh golden and shadowed the curves and hollows.

"Waitin' for him," Arch Linnbrook said in a terrible whisper. "Ain't even decent enough to wear a nightdress." Dropping her hair, he stepped back and she grabbed the blanket up around her with one hand. With the other she snatched up a small revolver, but Arch quickly took it away from her.

"Arch, listen to me—"

"Don't open your mouth again." Arch drew his revolver. "So help me God, I'll kill you both!"

Chapter Twenty

AT A CORNER table in Slager's, Con took a chair with Leroy Marcom of the Alliance Cattle Company. There was an unnatural quiet in the saloon, with the Texas men gathered in a tight knot at the far end of the bar. The Kansas Jayhawkers drank by themselves. The eyes of the Texas men were smoky in the lamplight as they watched the newcomers. But Con noted that Barney Slager had set out bottles and glasses for the new arrivals and was not refusing their Yankee money as payment.

"I have the feeling," Marcom said, watching Con, "that you may have tried to communicate with me about one of my partners, Bentley Hake. But communications being what they are, maybe the letters went astray."

Con felt uncomfortable, as if Marcom weighed him with suspicion. And he felt a faint anger mingled with his tiredness. He was remembering that this was the same table he had shared last year with the former major of the Union forces. When Marcom had made him a proposition. He wished at the moment he had never taken the job.

Stiffly Con outlined what had happened here in the Bend, how Hake was well on his way to rustling Jawbone blind.

Marcom's dark eyes in a rather narrow face watched him intently. "You seem to resent my presence," he said coldly.

"Not that," Con said, waving it off, "but I do want you to understand letters were written, but—" He told of Timoteo carrying letters to be mailed at San Pablo. How Timoteo was shot down.

"Well, it's unfortunate," Marcom said, lighting a cheroot. "But I've heard that the death of a Mexican in Texas is of minor importance."

Con gripped the edge of the table. "You'll make no friends around here with that attitude."

Con's voice was raised and the Jayhawkers looked around. Slager peered across the top of his bar. The Texans at the far end stood stiffly.

Marcom, noticing the stiffening silence, said, "Well, forget what I said, Jason. Let's get on with more important things. You have a plan for whipping Hake at his own game, I presume."

"For the moment I suggest you stay in town. There's the Jawbone room at the hotel for you. If there aren't enough rooms for the rest of them, they can bunk outside. Then in the morning—"

"Just a moment," Marcom snapped in his military voice. "Jawbone headquarters is only a few miles south. Why can't we ride there tonight?"

"You asked if I had a plan. I'm trying to tell you what it is. We'll leave town in the morning, head due south to the river. We'll recover the thousand head of cows Hake has already stolen and wipe out his crew as they ride in."

"Do you mean to say I've misjudged you!" Marcom's mouth stiffened out into the silky ends of his mustache.

"You mean why haven't I already done this? I'll tell you why. I've written for months, asking for a larger crew. But you chose to ignore it."

"I'm referring to this so-called strategy of yours. Why not go to Jawbone tonight and combine my men with the crew there. We'll have a formidable force."

"I don't think those men would join you, Marcom."

"Why not? I pay their wages!"

"That money won't buy loyalty in Texas," Con said, trying to keep the resentment of this man out of his voice. "Maybe in a year or so it will. But the war is too much in everyone's mind yet. Old hatreds die hard."

Marcom straightened in his chair, his square shoulders tight under the brown coat. "We have a few hatreds on our side, you know," he said caustically. "We didn't start the bloody mess, you know."

"That's a matter of opinion."

Frowning, Marcom took a drink. The horses at the rack in front of Slager's were stirring nervously. "Bentley Hake absconded with seven thousand dollars," Marcom said. "It was only luck that I checked his books. After that, I was only a few days behind him all the way to Texas."

"We'll get the stolen cows back and prevent any more from being taken."

"I wonder." Marcom eyed him with his chill gaze. "When a man is many hundreds of miles from his investment his perspective is sometimes faulty."

"Are you trying to say I've cheated you?" Con demanded.

"Let's say that I'm thinking out loud. Exploring every possibility."

"Explore and be damned then," Con said thinly.

"I am just surprised at your lack of eagerness to have your crew join with my men. It could be construed as an attempt to mislead me. To give Hake a chance—"

"If you think I'm working with that bastard—" Con was on his feet, his chair kicked back. The Jayhawkers at the bar wheeled to stare. The Texans moved into the deeper shadows so the enemy would have lamplight behind him.

Con, aware of the tension, said, "We could have a bloodletting in here, Marcom, if the talk gets out of hand."

"I just don't like being made a fool of," Marcom said, leaning back in his chair, the cheroot putting a shadow across his narrow face. "I just can't believe your men are as reluctant to fight as you make out."

Con waved a hand. "Look around this saloon, Marcom. Ask these men how they feel about it. They just spent some time telling me about it. In their eyes I'm a traitor to Texas. In your eyes I'm also a traitor."

"I didn't say that," Marcom snapped. "But you must admit your attitude in not wanting to go after Hake with a show of force gives me reason for doubt."

"One thing for sure," Con said bitterly, "I no longer belong at Jawbone."

As he started away from the table, Marcom warned, "You are under yearly contract to Alliance. The contract to be broken at our discretion, not yours."

"The hell you say."

Marcom got out of his chair, his face white. "You're still my employee. You'll take my orders."

"I have four hundred head of beef in my own name. I'll start moving them off Jawbone tomorrow."

"I would suggest we take stock of the situation at Jawbone," Marcom said, his voice chill, "before you try and move any of that group of cattle off land owned by Alliance."

"It's herd, not group of cattle."

"Yes, I know. But you see I don't pretend to be an expert in the cattle business. It's why my partners and I went in with Hake in the first place. He was the expert, or so he claimed. Remember what I said about moving that group of cattle you claim you own."

"*Claim* I own!" Con cried. "I do own them. I took most of my pay in cows, remember."

"I also know if there's been any mismanagement of Jawbone by you, then that beef is forfeit."

"You've been wrong on several points in the last few minutes," Con flung at him. "Believe me, you're dead on that point."

He started for the door and Marcom said, "Sergeant Smoot!"

The wide man with the shotgun stepped away from the bar. "Hold it, Jason," he ordered.

Con looked around at him, seeing the sweat on the square face. "Don't try it," Con warned. "This place will be filled with dead men before you take a deep breath."

"That's right," Barney Slager agreed, and from a shelf below the bar brought up a shotgun of his own. "You fight Yankees, Con, and we're for you."

"But don't make the mistake of turning them down, Barney," Con said. "If they want more whisky. You might lose out on some of those hard Yankee dollars."

Billy Snider said, "I warned you, Con. That you'd wake up one mornin' with a Yankee knife in your back."

Marcom looked around the room, forcing a smile. "The late unpleasantness of the war is over. So there's no need to dwell on the reasons we fought each other. My company is prepared to spend some money here. This town can grow with Alliance—"

Con didn't wait to hear any more.

He rode for Jawbone, knowing there was only one more thing for him to do in Texas—avenge Timoteo. He would do that and clear out. If he didn't there would be another senseless war like the last one. On a smaller scale, of course, but just as deadly to those involved. If this thing got out of hand it would be Texans on one side of the creek and Marcom and his Jayhawkers on the other.

When he had settled with Jud Kilhaven he would seek new fields. Fields not peopled by the ghosts of lost battles.

Chapter Twenty-one

CON RODE INTO the Jawbone ranch yard with the moon making it almost as bright as a Texas noon. He sat his saddle a moment, looking at the familiar buildings, knowing he was no longer a part of this. Jake Deward, on guard at the south end of the bunkhouse, came up. The man touched a match to a stub of cigar and the brief flare put a cold fire against his black beard. Con was telling him what had happened in town.

"Talk about a man caught in the middle," the one-eyed Jawbone hand said, "you're sure it, Con."

"Yeah. Marcom on one side and Hake and Kilhaven on the other."

"And don't forget Arch Linnbrook," Deward reminded.

And as Deward got out another match, Con said, "That's a fool stunt, striking a light when we're in a war."

Deward put the match back in his pocket. "Hake's after beef, not men. He won't come up here."

"Don't bet your life on it, Jake." Con wearily rubbed a

hand over his face. "How many of the boys will stick with me? At least till I can push my own cows off Jawbone."

"I'm with you, Con. The rest of the boys'll feel the same way. Them Yankee bosses got your tail in a knothole. And it'll make us plumb happy to fight 'em. Reckon you know for sure by this time that the war ain't over."

"So it seems."

"Alliance Cattle Company ain't no different than the Union Army. We're still Rebs and a Texas man is nothin' but scum to them boys."

"Jake, I'll need somebody I can trust. You're the one."

"What you want, Con?"

"Will you take the Whitley girl to town? See that she stays in the hotel until the westbound comes through. Then put her on it. Tell her to stay at the Drovers Hotel in Paso until I can get in touch with her."

"Sure, Con. But I got not one Jeff Davis dollar to my name."

"Get the money from Barney Slager. I should have done it myself, but there's been so damn many things happening— Tell Barney I'll stand good for it." Con's mouth tightened. "After all, it was his brother-in-law that got her into this fix."

Head bent in thought, he walked up to the house. He fumbled a match with which to light a lamp. As he opened the door he saw a blocky shadow. The short hairs tightened at the back of his neck. He was reaching for his gun when he was struck head on by a human avalanche.

So sudden was the attack that he was swept out into the yard. Dazed, he found himself on his back. Arch Linnbrook's solid weight pinned him.

"You've got her!" Arch cried. "Welcome to her. If you ever live long enough to enjoy it!"

Beyond Arch's tough arm he saw Coralee, barefoot, in the doorway. She was just stuffing the tails of the boy's shirt into the waistband of her narrow-legged breeches.

"Con!" she cried as Arch's fingers began digging into his throat. "I tried to warn you. But he held a hand over my mouth." Turning in the direction of the bunkhouse, she screamed for help. But Arch's bellow had already brought the men piling out.

Even before they could reach the scene of battle she was gingerly streaking over the yard, pebbles and rock, in her bare feet. She clawed at Arch's long rust-colored hair, crying, "Let him up. Let him up!"

Con was fighting to unseat Arch from his straddling position. But it was like trying to move the side of a mountain. His head was beginning to clear, but above him he sill saw a blurred vision of Arch and there was a great ringing in his ears.

Again Coralee grabbed at Arch's hair. Removing one hand from Con's throat the big man slapped the girl aside. And this movement threw him a little off balance so that Con, with a great upward thrust, was able to topple him. As they fell apart Con managed to get in a looping right to the head. But as he struggled up Arch got him around the knees. They fell, breaking apart. They came to their knees, grappling, each clouting the other about the face.

"Stop them, somebody!" Coralee cried, but none of the men ringed about made any move to interfere.

"Reckon this has been buildin' for a long time," Sam Trench said, as the two men smashed their way across the yard and back again.

"Can't you *do* something!" Coralee demanded.

If any of the excited onlookers even heard her above the cries of encouragement, the thudding of fists, the grunts of the combatants they gave no sign. Dust kicked up by hard heels drifted like river mist toward the moon. A vicious smash under the heart drove Con against the house. So great was the shock that he hung there for a moment, unable to lift his hands. The taller, heavier Arch Linnbrook with the greater reach gave a low cry of victory and closed in. With his left he pinned Con against the wall. His right crashed until the skin folded back redly from one side of Con's face.

With a scream Coralee spun her way through the ring of shouting men. Catching the back of Arch's shirt, she tried to pull him away. "You beast!" she cried.

But she might as well have tried to dislodge a house from its cornerstones. All she succeeded in doing was to rip Arch's shirt from his broad sweating back. And all the while Arch was hammering at Con. The stiffening seemed to be going out of Con's kneecaps.

"Stop them!" Coralee cried again, and two of the men dragged her off Arch's back. "Arch doesn't understand!" she wailed. He's fighting because of me. Of *me!* And there's no need—"

"Don't matter none, miss, "Deward said, gripping her by the wrists. "When two men want to fight you don't mess with it."

"I suppose it's the Texas code!" she screamed at them scornfully, "to allow men to beat themselves to death over a woman who means nothing to either one of them."

"We're hopin' Con whips him," Deward shouted above the din. "But if we horned in Con would never forgive us."

"I suppose if Arch used a knife you still wouldn't step in and make him quit!"

"Then we would. Or we'd see that Con also had a knife. If they wanted it that way."

"You're nothing but butchers," and still she tried to pull free of the strong hands that held her. Then she gave it up and turned wide eyes on the combatants.

Con, vaguely aware of what had been going on between Coralee and the men, finally broke away from the wall. He ducked under a wild swinging fist and hit Arch in the midriff, skinning his knuckles on the edge of the man's brass belt buckle. A great whooshing of stale air, as if blown from the dregs of a sun-heated whisky jug burst from Arch. His eyes became all white as the eyeballs rolled up into his head. Sensing a chance to end this Con rushed in.

And he found himself lifted with blinding pain on the hard cap of Arch Linnbrook's up-crashing knee. Choking with nausea, Con fell, landing on his side. Arch drove a boot toe into his back. Aimed another at his skull.

Despite the glancing blow to his groin that partially paralyzed him, Con was able to duck the swinging boot. However, the sole of Arch's boot jarred his temple. He caught Arch by an ankle, dragging him down. Locked together they rolled across the ground, their fists digging into any exposed part of the body. At last they broke apart and rose, two big men, their breathing heavy, shirts clawed from backs. A knee was ripped out of Arch's pants.

"You bastard!" Arch cried with a great straining of breath. "I'll kill you for what you done!"

"Nothing was done, you blind fool!"

"You finish with my sister! Then you take my girl!"

"Liar!" Con cried.

"You deny that you an' Nelda—"

Con cut him off. "Shut you're mouth! It's your own sister's name you blacken!"

"You're the one blackened it!" Arch cried, and they circled, each looking for an opening.

"Arch, shut your goddam mouth!"

"You an' Nelda—"

"Your sister's alive, not dead like Timoteo!"

"I didn't kill him."

"No matter who, you're partly responsible."

'I got nothin' to do with Kilhaven."

"He's your friend," Con sneered. "Hake's friend."

"No friend of mine."

And they closed again, senselessly battering each other .Because senseless now was the only way Con could evaluate the brawl. At first the pain, the brutal transfer of his pain to another had enabled him to dissolve in violence the frustrations that had been plaguing him.

But now, as his first rage against Arch's sudden attack in the doorway subsided, he was acutely aware that his every breath had to be dedicated to simply staying alive. For he had known this "milk brother" of his for a lifetime. And he knew once that explosive temper was fully extended there was no earthly way to curb it. Save with the temporary oblivion of unconsciousness. Or a well-placed bullet. As you'd aim at the eye of the charging grizzly you had wounded, knowing your very life depended on your accuracy.

And now as they fought each other across the yard, scattering the men like a pair of snarling dogs in a hen yard, Con knew he was wasting the strength he would need.

Suddenly as he drew back from the plunging Arch, Con was aware of horsemen in the yard.

He shouted, "Arch—" But still the battering fists came at him. As he closed with Arch, breathing as if he'd run to the ends of the earth and back, he saw Leroy Marcom, and the wide shadow of Allan Smoot with the shotgun. And the Kansas men. Come out from town to catch his own Jawbone men flat-footed. Their arrival covered by the shouting, the shrill sounds of horses milling in the corrals, spooked by the sounds of the brawl, the sharp bite of the blood smell in their nostrils.

Moonlight ran down the gun barrels of the horsemen. The Jawbone men stood with hands lifted. Still watching the fight, but looking sober and a little worried.

Again Con tried to get Arch to call off this madness. But Arch was bent on destruction. Con used his fists until the knuckles felt as if he'd been beating them against sheet iron, with about as much effect. And still Arch bore in, his bloodied head tough as a bull's skull. Con swung at his chin, bringing the fist up with all the power of thigh and back muscles behind it. But he just grazed the target and nearly fell, he was so far off balance.

And still Arch came in, his arms whipping, trying to run over the shorter man. Con gave way, and suddenly stood his ground. His right met the onrushing Arch in one last desperate attempt. And this time the target was not missed. Arch fell forward as if the world had suddenly gone out from under him.

Chapter Twenty-two

REELING AWAY FROM the fallen Arch Linnbrook, Con looked at Marcom. The man had dismounted with his men. He stood stiffly, a revolver steady in his hand. "I'm taking over the management of this ranch," Marcom said coldly. "When I have replaced you with a good man, I'll return to Chicago."

Con didn't answer. There seemed to be no words left in him at the moment. Coralee had handed him a bandanna dampened under the yard pump. As he sponged his face a quick fear touched him. He was unable to bend his trigger finger. It was either broken or badly sprained.

Marcom let his gaze touch the faces of the men in the yard. "Any of you men interested in staying on the Jawbone payroll may remain. Those who find the firing of Con Jason as manager of this ranch unpalatable can clear out."

Jake Deward said, "I don't know what unpalatable means, but we sure as hell don't like it none."

"And take him with you," Marcom said, waving his gun barrel at the unconscious Arch Linnbrook.

Con managed to stiffen the kneecaps of his weary legs. "You're welcome to Jawbone," he grunted, and started to turn away.

Marcom said, "You're to remain in town until I make a thorough investigation of conditions here. It goes without saying you're not to touch the cattle you've taken as part payment for your services."

"You're playing right into Hake's hands."

"I daresay we'll be able to handle Mr. Hake," Marcom said thinly. "You men have ten minutes to get your gear out of here."

Allan Smoot, shotgun under his arm, said, "Might be a prime idea to send 'em out with no shells for their guns. Rebels like to shoot at a man's back in the dark."

Con wiped his swollen lips with the damp bandanna. "Marcom, if you listen to him, you'll start the war all over again."

"In case you don't know it," Marcom snapped, "this state of Texas is still enemy territory. You are not a part of the Union. If I choose I can have Federal troops here."

"I wouldn't advise that."

"I have every right to protect the interests of my company here in Texas." Marcom's eyes hardened. "You were hired to do a job. You failed."

"Just how?"

"I had a very interesting discussion in town after you left," Marcom said, watching him. "One of your neighbors, Miss Linnbrook, happened to be staying at the hotel."

"Oh, I see," Con said with a short laugh. "The woman scorned."

"She said she begged you not to go into this deal with Hake," Marcom went on. "And she said you involved her brother, who out of loyalty to an old friend—"
pointing at the unconscious Arch.

"A falling out among thieves?" Marcom asked.

"You better put those words back in your mouth and "That's her brother on the ground there," Con snapped, swallow them!" Con warned. "I've taken enough for one night!"

"I could hang you and this Linnbrook and feel justified in so doing."

"Just because you believe the lies of a woman."

"I'm not altogether sure I believe everything she told me. But I intend to investigate her charges. One thing for sure, you allowed Hake to already get away with a sizable group of Jawbone cattle."

"I intended to get them back."

"Don't try and lie out of it."

Jamming the bandanna into his hip pocket, Con tried to flex his right hand. The injured finger bent slightly, but sent pain like a hot wire up his arm. "Do one thing," Con said, waving a hand at Coralee, "see that this girl gets on a stage for Paso—"

"She's not my responsibility," Marcom stated. "Sergeant," he snapped, turning to Smoot, "see that they leave with unloaded weapons."

"That's a thing you'd better not try," Con said, and some of the Jawbone men nodded.

"You have a woman here," Marcom pointed out. "If she's hurt it will be on your conscience, not mine. I imagine that in being in the company of men like yourselves, she is quite capable of looking out for herself."

"You've come pretty close to insulting a lady—" And Con, his fists clenched, started forward. Smoot's shotgun swung up to cover him. He felt fingers gripping his shirt sleeve, and Coralee's whisper, "Don't—please don't."

He halted and Marcom said, "As a partner in Alliance Cattle Company I claim the right to order you off this land. To protect my life and the lives of my men. It is also within my right to see that you do not have the means for immediate retaliation."

Con slowly stiffened his tired shoulders. "Coralee," he said without looking around. "Get a horse and clear out. Wait for us in the cottonwoods."

"No" she cried. "You can't fight them. It will be suicide—"

"It'll be suicide anyway," Con said, "if we're turned loose without shells in our guns. That's all Hake would need if we happened to run into him."

"You've built Hake into a bogeyman," Marcom told him. "Of course Hake is a threat, but if you Texans had half the guts you brag about you'd have chased him out of the country by this time."

Con got Coralee by an arm, tried to push her away. But she only moved a few feet and then stood there. Again he told her to wait for him in the cottonwoods. Again she refused.

Marcom said, "You're trying my patience, Jason. Now you can ride out of here without weapons of any kind." He turned to Smoot. "Sergeant, disarm them."

And Smoot, the barrels of the shotgun under his arm slanting at the ground, started forward. Tension lay over the yard like a dust cloud.

Con started to lift his hands as Smoot approached, knowing he would have to give in because there was no possible way to resist. Not without the shedding of blood here. And he couldn't risk that with Coralee so vulnerable.

"We'll unload our guns," he said, "if that will satisfy you."

"It won't. You've gone too far." Marcom let a small smile of triumph stir the mouth under his mustache.

The first indication Con had that anything was wrong was when he saw Marcom stiffen suddenly, as if some hard object had touched a sensitive spot on his back. And directly behind the ex-major Con caught a glimpse of a white bandage and then Charlie Baston's drunken voice, "Had to watch my chance, Con. Sorry it took so long."

"Charlie, get his gun."

"I already got it."

Marcom's Jayhawkers were staring at Charlie Baston, who had made his silent approach in sock feet. Smoot had turned, and the shotgun was starting to lift. Con reached for his own gun, but the holster was empty.

Marcom said nervously, "Easy, men." His voice was tight.

Smoot said, "Don't let one man spook you, sir."

"It's my spine that will be shattered by his bullet," Marcom said irritably. "Not yours." His gaze swung to Con. "What is this, Jason? A stalemate?"

"Ride out with your men," Con said. "Head for town. Come back at daylight, not before. Your guns will be here."

Marcom's eyes hated him. "I suppose you know this act will make you an outlaw."

"So be it."

"You're throwing me off my own property."

"You'd better get one thing straight," Con said, and every word was spoken with effort. He wanted to lie down and close his eyes. "This is Texas, not Illinois."

He felt a gun pressed into his hand and Coralee's voice, "You dropped it in the fight."

Muttering his thanks, he cocked the weapon. "You'll get it front and back, Marcom. Better do what I said. Order your men to put down their guns."

"It seems our positions have been suddenly reversed." Marcom drew himself up. "I was going to allow you a certain leeway, Jason, but now—"

"You didn't sound much like it a minute ago."

"There was a possibility that after checking the books, I would allow you to claim a part of your cattle at least."

"And now?"

"I assess the entire group of cows as damages against this company you were paid to represent."

Charlie Baston's voice over Marcom's shoulder cut the ex-major off like the lash of a rope end. Baston made an indelicate remark, considering there was a woman present. But Coralee, standing at Con's side now, gave no indication she had even heard the *segundo*.

With the stack of their weapons in the yard giving off a metallic shine in the moonlight, Marcom and his men rode in the direction of Santa Margarita. They cast weird shadows against the barn wall as they passed, reminding Con of the nightmares he had suffered through in the war. The appearance of gigantic shapes with swinging sabers. Nothing more deadly than a saber. A man will face cannon without so much ice in his entrails as when he sees a man on horseback chopping at his head with a bright blade.

Charlie Baston, the heavy bandage on his right arm and shoulder stained with Texas dust, holstered his gun. He took a long pull from a bottle he fumbled from a hip pocket.

"I don't know how you got into this, Charlie," Con said. "But thanks."

"You sent me to town, remember?" Baston took another

drink, then told how he had slipped into Slager's by the rear door and heard the talk that Marcom, a Union major in the war, was going to run Con off Jawbone.

"He had himself a talk with Nelda." Walking over, Baston toed Arch, who lay on his back now, his bruised face turned toward the moonlit sky. "Arch an' his sister. Both outa the same dirty corral."

And for the first time Con did not defend the Linnbrooks.

Charlie Baston said, "I trailed them blue-bellies down here and watched my chance."

"You couldn't have come at a better time, Charlie."

Baston gave him a hard grin. "I told you that I was needed. One arm or not. Let's make a fort outa this place, Con. We can stand 'em off—"

"We'll have to pull out. We have no right here now."

Baston looked at him in amazement for a moment. "The hell we ain't got a right here. Your pa built this place."

"Marcom has the law on his side."

Baston gave a hoot of laughter. "Only law in Texas is for Texans."

"We've got to get out of here," Con warned. He reminded his men that town was only a few miles away. Marcom could rearm and come storming back before the sun rose. . . .

They rode south and west, Coralee, her face showing strain, at Con's side. Arch had not regained consciousness sufficiently to sit a saddle. They had tied him on the back of a roan. Charlie Baston finished his whisky and sent the bottle crashing against a rock, the sound startling the horses. He asked if anybody had a drink. Nobody had. He settled into a sullen silence. They entered the mountains and the stars began to pale.

It was two hours past sunrise when they swung down in Caballo Canyon in front of the old Jawbone lineshack.

Removing his hat, Con stared tiredly down into the canyon. His herd branded "C" for Carter, his mother's name, "C" for the first son Nelda was to give him, was gone. A faint haze of dust hung in the air at the south end of the canyon, in the general direction of Mexico.

Chapter Twenty-three

ARCH LINNBROOK HAD been fully conscious for the past hour or so. Now he sat on the ground, hands roped behind his back. His right eye was swollen shut. There were gashes on both cheeks. His mouth was unrecognizable, only an opening in his ruined face.

"Funny damn thing, Con," he said thinly. "I come over to your place last night to tell you we'd have to stick together. That I was wrong in trustin' Hake——"

"A little late for that, Arch."

"Yeah." Arch turned his good eye on Coralee who stood in the shade of the lineshack wall. "You sure preach a good sermon, Con. About not bein' a thief. Maybe you don't steal beef. But you steal wimmen."

Before Con could reply, Coralee stepped up, her mouth taut. "Con was kind enough to give me a place to sleep. That's all it meant."

"And you waitin' for him," Arch went on, choking on his rage. "Shameless. Without a square inch of cloth coverin' you."

Coralee flushed and the men standing around looked uncomfortable. "I had no night clothes," she said, her voice shaking. "I told you that. Rather than sleep in the garments I'd worn all day——"

Arch struggled to his feet pulled viciously at the ropes binding his wrists, then gave up. "When a man buys somethin' he owns it, huh, Con?"

Con made a cutting gesture, sensing what Arch had on his mind. "You sent her two hundred dollars. I'll see that you're repaid."

"Oh, no. I ain't sellin'. I bought her, an' by God——"

Con drew his gun, his lips white. "I'm almost sorry I brought you along."

"Then why in hell did you?"

"I don't feel I owe you anything now. But even so, if I'd left you unconscious in the Jawbone yard Marcom might have come back and hanged you. He talked about it."

138

Arch looked at him. "I don't remember nothin' about anybody named Marcom. Who's he?"

"Riders came in while we were fighting. I tried to get you to back off, but you wouldn't. And after you were unconscious— Well, you didn't hear what was said. Nelda accused me of going in with Hake. She said that I roped you into helping me. In case you don't know it, Marcom is one of the partners in Alliance."

"So I give much of a damn about that," Arch said, his good eye flaming. "Behind my back all the time with my sister. Now you an' Coralee. Stud hoss, ain't you?"

"I'm not going to beat my knuckles bloody again," Con warned. He cocked the gun and Coralee stepped between them. After a moment Con let down the hammer and he walked with her to the other side of the lineshack, away from his men, who had gathered around the cookfire Sam Trench had built. And soon there would be a breakfast of sorts. Sam Trench was slicing with a large knife the slab of bacon he had brought from headquarters.

Con got Coralee aside, staring at the moving ball of dust in the distance. "I didn't want to bring you with us," he told her. "But I couldn't risk sending you to town."

"I understand."

"This is a pretty rough bunch of men for a girl to be around."

"My father ranched in Missouri once. I'm not a stranger to men like this." She took her gaze from his bruised face and pointed at the dust cloud moving south. "Bentley Hake stole your cattle."

"I can move faster than he can with the herd. I'll catch them at the river."

"You look dead tired. You're in no condition for a fight."

He clenched his right hand. The pain was still in that all-important trigger finger. He felt cold sweat against his back. She was right. He was in no condition to fight. But everything he had in the world was tied up in that herd of cattle.

"We'll eat," he said. "Then I'll decide what to do about you."

After the meal Con gave his orders. Charlie Baston and Sam Trench were to stay behind and guard Coralee here at the lineshack. And keep Arch a prisoner.

"If Arch makes trouble," Con said, "kill him. God knows I feel like it right now."

Arch, sitting on the ground, his wrists tied, only glared at him.

Coralee gave Con a strange look. "No matter what he's done, you can't talk of killing him in cold blood."

"I should kill him now and be done with it. That's the sensible thing to do. But I'm giving him this chance. Maybe it's more than he'd give me. I don't know."

Charlie Baston stormed up. "Your plan sounds right," he said, his eyes bright with fever. "All except for me. I'm ridin' with you. Leave Dave Rubel behind with Trench."

"Charlie, you do what I say and no argument," Con snapped. "I've got enough on my mind."

But when it came time to ride, Baston stubbornly went on ahead. Spreading his hands, Con said, "What's the use?" He told Rubel to stay behind with Trench, then gave both men their final instructions.

When he was ready to ride, Coralee turned to him, her blue eyes moist. "You're a hard and bitter man. Maybe there are some things about you I could never understand. But I do know you're short-handed. You need every man. I can stay here alone. Just give me a rifle. I can use one."

"You do what I say." He gave her a tight smile.

"Why is it a woman is supposed to obey without question?"

"A man knows more about danger than a woman."

She looked at him for a moment. Then she lifted herself and kissed him on the mouth. The men were suddenly interested in the funnel of dust bearing south toward Mexico. Arch, his ruined face bright with anger, glared at Con.

As they rode out Con looked back. Coralee lifted a hand. He acknowledged it.

Con said to no one in particular, "I hope I've done right. If anything happens to her—" Then he saw Charlie Baston waiting for them, gray about the mouth now, sickness deep in his eyes. "You never could take orders, Charlie. Damn it, why do you make things even tougher for me?"

"Go to hell," Charlie Baston muttered. "Once I get me some rustler whisky I'll be a new man."

Chapter Twenty-four

As HE RODE Con wondered just what his feelings were toward his men. They had hedged about helping him, when as foreman-manager of Jawbone, he had attempted to protect the interests of his Yankee employers. But now that his own herd was threatened they were eager to risk their necks for him. It was loyalty, no mistake about that. But still he could not help but resent the fact that even though they were helping him now, the whole range was in danger of blowing up. And they were partly responsible. Their refusal to act had turned Marcom against him. Because even though Nelda had admittedly put a vengeful knife in him, so to speak, Marcom's suspicions were already sufficiently aroused, his mind conditioned to accept just about anything said against Con. . . .

Where the river curved back cool and green from the eastern tip of the rim there was a notch in the bleak hills on the American side. Here was a ford that enabled a horseman or cattle to make a reasonably safe crossing during periods of low water. But now the river was high, due to the spring runoff in the New Mexico mountains. As it had many times before, Con's knowledge of the country saved many miles of travel over well-marked cattle trails. Con took his men high into the Chisos, then abruptly down what appeared to be almost a sheer cliff; a switchback trail he and Arch had used years back. A trail better suited to mules than to horses, but they made it to the brushy dome of a hill on the west side of the gap and above the river. Only one horse fell during the descent, and that belonged to a Jawbone man named Reynolds. It rolled but the man was able to spring clear. Thereafter the horse limped, but it could still carry the rider.

In the sparse shade afforded by an overhang of rock, they waited. It was stifling on the hills and within a matter of minutes their clothing was soaked with sweat. Charlie Baston lay on his back, breathing heavily, hat over his eyes. And when Con crept close to ask how he was, there came to his nostrils an unmistakable odor that lifted the hair at the back of the neck. The odor associated with battlefields. Gangrene.

"Charlie, how do you feel?"

Baston got his eyes open. He looked around a little wildly, then his gaze settled on Con. "My arm hurts like hell."

'Damn it," Con said, and a feeling of helplessness engulfed him. "Why didn't you stay at Doc's like I told you?"

Charlie Baston shook his head. "Your poppa an' Big Ed need me. An' you need me, boy."

Con swallowed, and the men gathered around, looked at the gray-faced Baston on the ground. They looked questioningly at Con. There was no perspiration on Baston's forehead. It was dry as sun-baked paper.

"I shouldn't have let him come," Con said through his teeth. "Why didn't I knock him out like I did in town? And tie him to a saddle and take him to Doc Maxfield?"

Deward said, "If you'd taken time to done that Hake would have your cows clean to Chihuahua City before you seen their dust again."

"What's a few head of cows?" Con worked on his trigger finger, trying to get the stiffness out. "Every damned thing I try to do is wrong." He put a hand to his face, feeling the raw places where Arch's fists had battered him.

Charlie Baston struggled to put an arm under him. "Con, I'll talk to your poppa. It wasn't right for him to burn them books. It was your hoss to trade for them books, if you wanted."

Kneeling down, Con pushed him against the ground. "Soon as Hake's men come with the cows we'll get whisky. We'll get some if it means we have to kill every one of them."

"Won't do no good to fret now, boy. Your poppa hung the Abolitionist fella. I cut him down myself."

"Oh, God," Con groaned and closed his swelling eyes. He looked around, his lips nearly as gray as Baston's face. "Who's got a belt knife?" The men exchanged glances. None of them carried any steel.

Jake Deward said, "Won't do no good to take the arm. He's too far gone. I seen 'em like this in the war."

"I didn't ask for your opinion!" Con snapped, and his nerves were so played out that he was on the point of smashing

Deward in the face. Then he half turned away. "I'm sorry, Jake."

"Know how you feel, but God knows you tried to get Baston to let the Doc take care of him. Ain't your fault."

"There was only one virtue my father had that I can remember," Con said quietly, staring to the river below and to the opposite bank where thick willows screened Vega Verde. "He took care of his own. A Jawbone man in trouble meant Poppa shared that trouble."

"You got to make up your mind, Con," one of the men said. "Hake and them boys will outnumber us three to one. You can't worry about Charlie Baston and get your cows back all at the same time."

Con pushed his hand to his gun, aware of the pain in fingers and thumb. He was so pitifully slow. With the blued steel weapon in his palm, he checked the loads. Then he reholstered the gun.

"You boys wait here," he said. "I'm going across the river."

"For God's sake, what for?" Deward demanded.

"For some whisky. And a knife." He looked them over, his gaze sliding to each dust-caked face in turn. "Follow orders this once, boys. It's all I ask. Keep Charlie quiet. I figure the herd is about five miles north. I hope I'm right. With any luck I'll be back and we'll have the job on Charlie's arm done before Hake and his boys get here."

"We'll have to have a fire and a hot iron to stop the bleedin'. They'll see the smoke."

"Then they'll see the smoke," Con said, and started away, but Deward said, "I'll go with you."

Con turned. "You don't have to, Jake. It's risky as hell."

"Ain't nobody says I got to do anything." Deward carefully removed a half-smoked cigarillo from his shirt pocket, shoved it between his bearded lips. "But I'm goin' all the same."

"The rest of you keep Charlie quiet," Con said. "If we don't get back, let the herd go. As soon as Hake swims it across you head back for the lineshack. See that the girl gets on the stage for Tucson and has a little extra to get her started there."

"Ain't a ten-dollar gold piece between us," Reynolds said. The side of his face was scraped when his horse had rolled.

Con walked over to where Charlie Baston lay. Baston said nothing as Con went through his pockets. Con came up with a leather sack tied to the belt, and hidden under the shirt. "Charlie won this off Mark Dollop. And Dollop stole it from the girl."

"The hell you say," Deward exclaimed.

Con looked in the sack. There was a little over three hundred dollars. He threw the sack to Reynolds. "I'm trusting you," he said.

"You'll be back," Reynolds said. "But if you ain't— Well, you got my word about the girl."

Con and Deward put their horses into the river some distance below the ford, swimming them, hanging to the bushy tails. They came up on the south bank where the willows were thick. They checked their guns for moisture. They stood there a moment, teeth chattering from the cold water. Deward had lost his eyepatch. His left eye socket was an ugly place in his face. He pressed river water from his beard. Both men emptied their boots.

Tying their horses in the willows, they crept forward; south of the collection of mud and pole shacks could be heard the lowing of cattle. The thousand head Hake had already rustled from Jawbone. And smaller bunches picked up since the main raid had been made. There was no way of knowing how many men were in camp. Probably some left behind, Con reasoned, to keep an eye on the herd.

But no matter what the odds, he had to get that knife. Even though in the back of his mind a voice said that he was already too late. That there was nothing that could be done to save Charlie Baston's life. Due to the man's own foolishness.

But I've got to try and save him, Con thought. I've got to *try*. If I don't I could never live with myself.

Giving Deward a signal, they moved up to the edge of the clearing. Five saddled horses were tied to a rail of a makeshift corral beyond the last of the half-dozen shacks in a semicircle about a large fire ring.

A murmur of voices reached them. Keeping to the trees they moved behind the nearest shack. From here they could look between two of the crude structures, past the fire ring. Just this side of the sun-streaked river they could see four men playing some sort of card game on a blanket spread on the ground. Hats tipped back, the men sat around the blanket, intent on their cards.

Five horses and four men, Con thought. One man not accounted for.

If he had any luck Con hoped to be able to find a knife in one of the shacks, and maybe some whisky. At least he had to have the knife. They'd have to tie Charlie Baston down. The thought put cold sweat down his back.

The nearest shack was empty. Only a cot made of poles, covered by moth-eaten Saltillo blankets. The second shack had occupants. Con threw a big shadow in the doorway. He saw a girl on her knees, her back to the door, long dark hair loose about the shoulders of a red dress. She was stroking the face of a man with a pale beard. Traxton, who once had taken Con's bullet in a boot heel. Traxton was smiling at the girl.

She giggled and Traxton, wearing no shirt, said, "I'll buy you the Mexican moon when we get to Chihuahua—" And at that moment he looked over the girl's shoulder and saw the gun in Con's hand. Traxton's face did not change expression.

"Easy," Con whispered.

But a tremor went through the girl. She looked around, sprang to her feet. An ear-splitting scream broke from her lips. Traxton gave a cry of warning, and swept up a gun from under ragged Saltillo blankets. The hammer came crashing down. But the bullet went through the mud and willow ceiling. Con's gun had jumped in his bruised hand. Traxton settled back, part of his jawbone embedded in the willow poles at his back.

There was firing outside, the sounds of men running. The hysterical girl continued to scream, the back of a hand against her teeth. She bit into it and blood ran down over her chin.

Outside, hugging the shack wall, Deward fired into the willows. A man cried out. Con reached Deward's side, cut down on a lathy man just lifting a rifle. The man folded with a grunt of pain. A third man had moved so quickly his spurs became tangled up in the blankets. Cards and chips went flying. He fell headlong, and Deward shot him through the top of the skull.

The fourth member of the group ran along the river bank,

his hat flying off. He turned, firing once, lost his balance and fell in a pool. He floundered and Deward lifted his gun, but Con knocked his arm down. "That's enough, Jake," he said.

"Should've let me kill him," Deward said, and spat out his cold cigarillo.

"I don't have much of a stomach for bloodletting," Con said.

The rustler in the pool made some wild thrashing movements, was caught by the current and sucked out into midstream. For a moment all Con could see was his lifted hand. Then that too went under.

"You're a queer one, all right," Deward said. "You think that fella wouldn't have done you in? Had it been you in the river instead of him?"

"Very likely. Let's get out of here. There may be more men guarding the herd."

Con found a bottle of whisky beside the man Deward had shot through the head. One of the dead rustlers wore a long-bladed Mexican *cuchillo*. Con shoved this in his belt and put the whisky in his saddlebags when they got back to their horses.

They went back across the river, soaking themselves again. This time the current carried them half a mile or so downstream from the ford. And barely did they have Texas sand under their boots than there was a sudden rattle of gunfire from somewhere up the gap. And through the willows Con saw the first of what appeared to be an immense herd plunge bawling into the river.

Chapter Twenty-five

BENTLEY HAKE FELT the stinging dust in his nostrils, felt it turn to mud upon his sweating face. As the cattle filed down the draw toward the river, he drew in a bay horse and from a ledge watched them pass. It was ironic in a way, he thought with satisfaction, that four hundred of the nearly thousand head of beef being driven south belonged to Con Jason. He could never forget that Jason had been the one to kill

Homer Peale. And now Hake needed the dead man's peculiar talents, the ability to copy handwriting. Well, he would have to make up his own bill-of-sale for these cows and present it when Don Bricido Canales took over the herd in Chihuahua.

Below him Jud Kilhaven was shouting at the men to round up the stragglers. Rope ends popped as the men used their spurs. Tired horses lunged, cows squealed as the rope ends stung their rumps. Then Kilhaven seeing Hake on the ledge wheeled and came up.

"Good day's work," he said, and cuffed back his hat and lazily began to roll a cigarette while his muddy-brown eyes watched the progress below.

"How long, Jud?" Hake demanded, his dark eyes, showing strain from dust and glare, touching his brother's long face. "The quicker we're moving toward Chihuahua the better I'll like it."

"Another week oughta do it," Kilhaven said. He touched a match to his cigarette and his gaze ran over the other man's torn white shirt, his black broadcloth pants shoved into boots that no longer bore a high polish; now they were gouged from brush and liberally coated with dust. "You don't look so fancy now," he observed.

Hake turned in the saddle, his mouth hard. "There's a certain need for what you call fancy attire in business like this."

Kilhaven gave him a lazy smile. "I s'pose."

"You act like you have a rock in your boot. Let's hear the complaint."

"Ain't no complaint," Kilhaven drawled. "I just admire how them fancy clothes and that smile of yours gets us all this good life." He waved a brown hand at the cattle streaming south with horn clicking, hoofs raising a great cloud of dust. "Settin' a saddle from first light to last. Wonderin' ever' time you look over your shoulder if some Texan ain't goin' to be there with a rope."

"For God's sake, they've forgotten all about you killing that Mexican. Arch said they already hanged one man for it. Isn't that enough?"

"Speakin' of Arch, them fancy clothes, that fancy talk didn't do you much good with his sister."

"Good enough."

"You never stayed long up at her place."

"I stayed as long as I wished," Hake said impatiently.

"I was there long enough too," Kilhaven said. A lazy grin slanted across his face.

"I suspected that. And just how did it happen?"

"Me, a dirty old Quantrill man. No fancy talk, no fancy clothes. I just whispered in her ear and that was it. I scared the hell out of her. She figured I'd tell Con Jason she'd got herself a husband up in Missouri once."

"You had a good teacher," Hake said shortly. "Quantrill had a talent for scaring the hell out of most people."

"Me, ridin' the brush with old Charley Quantrill. With half the country lookin' for us. And you livin' like the King of England on a big gold hoss. Up there in Chicago."

"I was a prisoner of war," Hake said bluntly.

"I heard how they treated you. A Southern gentleman, they said you was. That's where you met Marcom and them other Yankees. Couldn't do enough for you. Takin' you outa the stockade on weekends. Lettin' you eat in their houses and look their wimmen over."

"So that's what's ailing you," Hake said. "Just what would you have had me do? Turn my back on them when they tried to do me a favor?"

"Reckon not. But I had to get it outa my system. Galls a man when he lives in the brush like an animal—"

"From all reports there was a lighter side to Quantrill's activities," Hake said dryly. "Ever keep track of the women you boys rode off with?"

"We didn't always ride off with 'em," Kilhaven said with a slow grin. "Most times we took 'em where we found 'em."

Hake jerked low the dusty brim of his black hat. "Worry about women when we get to Chihuahua City. But let me warn you. Try any of those Quantrill tricks down there and they'll cut you down the middle and throw you into a slow fire."

"You won't have no trouble, that's for sure. You'll get yourself some more fancy clothes and—"

"I've heard enough of this. We've got a herd to move. Let's get at it."

"I just figure I ain't as fancy as you, boy," Kilhaven said.

"I figure that sometimes I got to take the leavin's. You get there first, maybe, but I figure to get there second."

"Just what are you driving at?"

"I'm thinkin' of that gal you come here with from Saint Looey. Coralee Whitley."

Hake gave a small laugh. "Much as I hate to admit it, I didn't make much progress there."

"I don't believe you worth a damn. I just want you to know that before we quit this country, I aim to ask her just how much progress you made."

"We've got work to do. Forget chasing that girl."

"I don't aim to chase her none. I aim to take her with us."

"Do what you want, but you're wasting your time with her."

"You mean 'cause she's a lady and wouldn't even give me the dust I could wipe off her shoe?"

"You can try, but you'll have to kill her first."

Kilhaven shook his head. "I bet you one of them Mex silver-mounted saddles against a busted spur that 'for we get to Chihuahua City she'll run nekkid through cactus if I say so."

"Women will one day be the death of you, Jud," Hake said.

"They ain't been the death of you yet."

"There's a difference between what could be called persuasion and the methods you use."

"I get me some fancy clothes in Chihuahua an' slick my hair back with some smellin' stuff and maybe I can use some of that persuasion."

"Jud, every damn time we try to work together it ends up like this. I'm sick of it."

Jud Kilhaven, laughing, started to rein away from his brother. Below the last of the herd had gone by, lifting a great funnel of dust. There was a sudden rattle of gunfire in the direction of Vega Verde across the river.

Kilhaven twisted around in the saddle. "Trouble."

Hake was about to say something sarcastic, to the effect that his brother shouldn't worry about gunfire. Not when there were more important topics to discuss; the age-old feud had started when they were boys. A girl back home saying,

"Your brother is a pig, Bentley. Why can't he be a gentleman like you?" And Jud hearing it.

At that moment the rider Hake had left to watch their backtrail came pounding south, hat brim pushed back by the force of his riding.

"Hake!" he shouted, pointing north. "Twenty-one men comin'. I counted 'em!"

"Texans," Hake said, his bloodshot eyes scanning the sky to the north.

The rider shook his head. He was one of those who had formerly worked for Arch Linnbrook at 88. "Never seen this bunch before, Hake," the man said. "Nobody from around here."

Hake leaned forward, the horn pressing against his taut belly. "Could you tell who seemed to be in command?" When the man nodded, Hake said, "Describe him."

A thin-faced man with a mustache that curved down, the rider said. A man who sat his saddle as if he had iron pipe for a spine, his back was that straight. And beside him rode a very thickly built man who carried a shotgun.

Hake licked at the dust on his lips. "I knew Marcom would come," he said, peering north. "I didn't think it would be this soon."

"Reckon he seen our dust," Kilhaven said. "What now?"

"We'll get across the river and make a stand there. Marcom is so certain of his invincibility that he'll likely try to take his men across. We'll cut him to pieces if he tries."

Shouting, they joined the drag of the herd, waving their hats, hurrying the frantic cows who pushed on against those ahead.

"Not too fast," Kilhaven warned. "They'll run sure as hell."

"Let them," Hake said to his brother as they swung their horses back and forth across the drag.

"Reckon you never seen a stampede by a river," Kilhaven snapped. "You'll have dead cows stacked ten feet high."

There came a scattering of shots behind them, the bullets falling far short of the mark.

"Just like Marcom to waste shells," Hake said.

Through the dust ahead Hake could see the vanguard of the herd plunging into the river. Riders were swimming their horses, trying to keep the cows from milling. And suddenly from a brushy hilltop that jutted abruptly from the river bank, Hake saw a grizzled man rise up. The man had lost his hat and his gray-streaked hair curved down to frame his wide face. His shirt was gone and his right shoulder and arm were packed with filthy bandage.

"Comanches!" the man shouted and fired a revolver down into the herd.

"It's that loco Charlie Baston!" Kilhaven shouted. "Thinks we're Indians!" Snapping his rifle from the boot he sent a shot winging upward. But he fired in haste, and the bullet went far to the right. Baston was firing down into the herd again and a cow reared with a great bellow of pain. As it came down its horns slashed the flank of the animal directly ahead. This cow lunged, climbed up the back of another. For a moment the cows seemed to mill uncertainly, then they put down their heads and began to run. The ground shook and the dust was thicker than a river fog.

Kilhaven took one final moment to finish the job at hand. His next shot caught Charlie Baston in the chest, turning him. The man came rolling down the slope, straight into the churning mass of cattle. Kilhaven saw other men on the hill now, firing down. He got off another shot; one of them fell back. Then he had to run for his life.

Chapter Twenty-six

CON, HIS CLOTHING plastered to his bruised and tired body, scrambled into the saddle when he saw the lead cows go plunging into the river. Shouting at Deward to follow, he set his spurs and they sent their horses along the sandy shore, following a trail of sorts through the willows. When they were fifty yards from the gap Con caught a glimpse of dirty white on the hill he had left. His heart dropped like a ball of lead.

"Charlie!" he shouted. But he knew his voice was wasted in the crash of gunfire, in the roar of the herd. He saw one of his Jawbone men try to drag Charlie Baston back to shelter. But the *segundo* shook him off and yelled something

Con could not hear. Baston fired down into the herd. And in a matter of seconds the whole gap was filled with rearing cattle. Then they began to run right over those cows already in the river. He saw Charlie Baston make a slow somersault through the air, strike the back of a lunging steer, hang there for a moment. Then disappear under the driving hoofs.

Three riders, swimming their horses frantically away from the avalanche, were headed for the strip of beach where Con and Deward had pulled back their mounts. Ahead the shore was blocked by the flood of cattle.

The three men in the river saw Con and Deward. As they sent their horses lunging up the bank, they fired their rifles. Con's long gun knocked a man down. His second shot hit a horse.

The third man tried to fire his rifle, but evidently the cartridges had become fouled by river water. He threw the rifle away and tried to reach his revolver. Deward shot him.

Two more rustlers, trying to reach shore, never made it. Men and horses disappeared under the tide of brown hides reaching far out into the river.

And when the river itself was blocked by the cows dead or dying, the rest of the herd swung right and left along the north shore of the river. Under the sheer weight of numbers spindly willows snapped like matchsticks. To his right Con saw a ledge of sand some four feet high. Signaling for Deward to follow, he sent his frightened horse up the bank. He turned. Deward almost made it but a rustler, unhorsed, clambered out of the river. He fired a revolver into Deward's back. The one-eyed man plunged down, and the herd went over him and in an instant engulfed the horse he had been riding. And also the rustler who had shot him.

The herd swept past, some of them spilling into the river below. Moving slower now, their momentum slackening. An island of brown moved slowly in the center of the river. Occasionally a steer head raised, horns flashed briefly in the sunlight. Then it went under.

Sickened by what he had seen this day, Con sat dejectedly in his saddle, the stillness that followed gunfire almost awesome. The waste of life. All because of the greed of one man, Bentley Hake.

Slowly he rode toward the gap, and where the sand bank

began to crumble underfoot he was forced to dismount and lead his tired horse. He came to the gap and the floor was littered with the bodies of steers, of horses, of men. There seemed to be no one left alive. He had trouble holding his horse in as he rode up the draw a few yards and saw the thing in the sand. All that was recognizable was a piece of dirty white cloth that had once been a bandage.

Con removed his hat and the sun beat on the tangle of wet hair, felt fiery against the back of the shirt soaked from two crossings of the river.

Leroy Marcom's voice reached him as if from a great distance. "I just can't quite decide where you fit into this, Jason."

Con looked around, saw Marcom sitting stiff in the saddle, his left arm hanging crookedly. Blood dripped from the ends of his fingers. Beside him was Smoot, shotgun resting across the saddle pommel. His Jayhawkers had swung down and were looking around at the carnage, shaking their heads.

Con said, "Did you get Hake and Kilhaven?"

"They must have crossed the river," Marcom said, his voice edged with pain. He nodded at the trampled body and the piece of dirty white cloth. "One of your men?"

"One of mine." Slowly, with Smoot watching him, Con removed the sheath knife from his belt. He dropped it beside Charlie Baston. From his saddlebag he took the half-filled bottle of rustler whiskey. He took a long drink, then he smashed the bottle on a rock.

"Is this some sort of symbolism?" Marcom said in his tight, military voice.

"I was going to have to cut off his arm."

"Probably better this way," Marcom said. "An amputation in the field without proper facilities—"

Con said, "Hake stole my herd. I trailed it here. I'm going to round it up. Are you going to try and stop me?"

Marcom looked at him. The pain from his shattered arm showed on his face. "We saw their dust. Lucky for you we got here. I guess those left have fled across the river."

Con's men had come down from the hill, and it was a bad moment.

"A bitter pill for my boys to swallow," Con said. A hard

smile touched his lips. "Yankees helping to pull us out of the fire."

"When we returned to town last night," Marcom said, "unarmed—" He looked angry for a moment at memory of the humiliation. And then pain or tiredness, Con couldn't tell which, seemed to take the steel-bright glitter from his eyes. "I found that Miss Linnbrook had left a message for me. Something to the effect that what she had told me earlier was perhaps a lie. *Perhaps,* she said."

"At least she must have put doubt in your mind. But she couldn't go all the way and confess her lie. Well, I thank her for that gesture toward honesty."

Marcom looked around at the Jawbone men, two of them without hats, one with a rifle, the rest with revolvers. Four men left. "Maybe you boys will have a good word to say about Yankees now." Marcom tried to smile.

The men just looked at him. And one of them spat contemptuously.

"Someday the war will really be over," Con said. "But it will take a while."

"I'm still a little in doubt as to just how I should classify you, Jason," Marcom said. "Your presence here and all the evidence could mean that you tell the truth. That Hake did steal your group of cattle."

"Yes, he stole my group," Con said, his tone biting. "He also stole your group. I hope there's enough left of my group to round up."

"We'll give you a hand, Jason," Marcom said, "then we'll go after Mr. Hake. It will be my pleasure to hang him." He turned to Smoot. "Sergeant, I seem to have contracted a slight wound. A bandage would be in order, I think."

"Right away, sir."

Chapter Twenty-seven

CON RUBBED A hand over his face. Sweat stung the cuts put there by Arch Linnbrook's knuckles. He lowered the hand, put on his hat. He was facing north. Something on the steep trail they had descended earlier in the day caught his eye. A rider. Bent over the horn. He was hatless and even from this distance Con could see the long rust-colored hair. A big man. Arch Linnbrook.

Something caught at his throat when he thought of Arch, a prisoner at the old lineshack. Left with Sam Trench and Rubel. And here was Arch. A free man. Either by his own hand, or someone else's.

Without a word Con sent his horse lunging up to the crown of the hill where Charlie had made his last defiant gesture; and somehow, Con thought, it was the same sort of foolhardy thing his own father and brother had done. Charging Yankee cannon with their sabers.

Halfway down the switchback trail along the face of the cliff, Arch had dismounted. He was sitting on a wide ledge of rock, his horse standing with trailed reins. Arch held both hands to his stomach.

"I spotted you comin', Con," he said, his voice so low that Con had to kneel beside him. "I'm so damn tired. I sat down to wait."

"How'd you get loose?" Con had drawn his gun, his mouth a vicious line across his face. "Is Coralee all right?"

Arch's face was swollen so from the beating last night that he was almost unrecognizable. One eye was swollen shut. He had only partial vision out of the other. "Sam Trench brung a slab of bacon along from Jawbone. We had it for breakfast."

"Never mind that—"

"Sam left the knife he sliced it with stickin' in the table. I got into the shack and rubbed them ropes on the blade. Then I took the knife." Arch was gasping now. "Sam had his back turned. I got him. That crazy Dave Rubel tried to shoot me. I never was much of a knife-thrower, but I got him in the throat."

"You—" Con started to curse him, then broke off. "Where's Coralee?" he demanded.

"I was bringin' her here. Goin' to cross the river here. Paid two hundred dollars— Wasn't goin' to let you have her—"

"Where—is—she?" Con cried, and caught Arch by a shoulder and shook him. Arch fell over on his side. Before he had been hunched over and Con had not seen the extent of his wound. But now he saw that the whole lower half of

Arch's shirt was stained, as were his canvas pants. "They run into me about two miles back. Hake an' Kilhaven. Kilhaven shot me. Left me for dead."

"They've got Coralee!"

"Yeah. Took her from me. They figure to swing nawth, then head into Mexico over by Agua Negro. I heard 'em talkin'. They figure to get another bunch an' come back—" A shudder touched Arch. He slanted his swollen eye at Con. "Everything gone wrong, Con. You was right. I never should've listened to Hake—"

His body stiffened and his spurs clanked a few times against the rocky ledge.

For only a moment did Con look down on this stranger. A man he did not know. Not the Arch Linnbrook of the old years before the war. Maybe, as Nelda had said once, the war had changed everything and everybody.

He rode on up the switchback trail and at the top he looked back. Already the roundup of the cattle had begun. He turned his horse north. He wondered then how much forgiveness could be left in a man. Arch, mortally wounded, had stayed in the saddle long enough to tell Con that Coralee was a prisoner. And on the other hand it was Arch himself who was responsible for her present danger.

It was two hours before he saw their dust. They had swung past the old lineshack in Caballo Canyon. And he knew the reason. They had taken the comparatively fresh horses belonging to Sam Trench and Rubel. And left their own sweat-streaked mounts. One of them, a roan, had an ugly slash across its right foreleg, likely from the fight at the river.

He found Sam Trench lying face down by the shack door. The ugly wound between the shoulder blades told how he had died. In the clearing lay the round-faced kid, Dave Rubel. There was a great stain from the jugular, which the thrown knife still embedded in his throat had severed.

Con felt a churning in his stomach. He retched and weaved a moment. Then he climbed back into the saddle. Two good men dead because of Arch. He pushed his horse along the trail. Unless he had luck he'd never catch them now. His horse wouldn't last another five miles if he pushed it. They would have left him far behind by nightfall.

Coralee! The thought of what might have happened to her

ran through him like ice. He rode, bloodshot eyes always on the hoofprints that led north. Cursing Arch one minute for turning into a cold-blooded killer. Thanking him silently the next, for hanging on long enough to give the word about Coralee.

The trail now veered toward the west, through the foothills of the Chisos. Con had no idea how long he traveled. But he knew the sun was in his eyes now instead of at his back.

After what seemed like hours he came upon a dead bay horse. It was branded Jawbone and he remembered it as the one Coralee had ridden last night to the lineshack. It had been shot once in the flank. The second shot had been fired into the head from close range. Con pushed on, a faint hope building in him now. In his tired mind he tried to reconstruct what had happened. The bay had suffered the flank wound and being of no further use had been killed. But what had happened to Coralee?

Half-fearfully he thought of turning back to the dead horse and searching the brush for her body. But he wouldn't let himself even consider the possibility that she might be dead.

And soon his tired eyes, focused on the tracks in the dust, picked up the change of pace in the two horses ahead. Two instead of three now. One mount carried double. He came to a place where they had changed horses. He could see the narrow prints of a woman's boot in the soil. For some distance she would ride with one of them, and then with the other. So as to distribute the load between the horses.

He pushed on, his horse beginning to founder now despite the slow and steady pace he had been holding it to. He could feel the tremor of its great body, hear the gasping for air. Foam flecked its muzzle, blew back into his own face. He wiped it away.

A breeze had come up, blowing strong in his face. That was good, he thought. He could approach and their mounts would not catch his scent. Good, good, good—the thought kept spinning around in his mind. All that had happened in a space of hours had drained him. The lack of sleep, taking hasty meals wherever he could. The brawl with Arch last night. The fight at the river today—

And the worry over Coralee.

The voices came to him suddenly and for a moment they didn't register.

". . . the hell with that, fancy man. I'm keeping her. Understand?"

"It'll be your neck," Hake said, "if they catch you."

And Con was abruptly at the crest of a hill where the trail pitched down sharply into a shallow bowl. Junipers let the whining wind through their branches. Two Jawbone horses, heads down, stood with trailed reins a few yards from Hake and Kilhaven. Coralee sat on a deadfall, her hands tied. The two men eying each other belligerently. Both with belt guns. Hake not looking so fancy now. His hat was gone, his dark hair matted to his sweating forehead.

"Use your head, Jud," Hake was saying. "There'll be fifty women in Chihuahua City."

"Your deal's blown higher'n the moon."

"We can get another crew and come back."

Kilhaven shook his head, then looked at Coralee. "It's her fault we're shy a hoss."

"Then leave her—"

"She shouldn't have tried to make a break."

"You didn't have to shoot the horse. So it's your own fault."

"I aimed to scare her. The hoss got in the way. So she'll pay." Kilhaven's long face looked around at the girl again, seated stiffly on the deadfall. "You go on. I'll see you in Agua Negro."

And his gaze traveled upward to the brushy lip of the hill and he saw Con Jason.

While they had been talking, Con swung down. The gun in his stiffened right hand seemed to have the weight of a bucket of stones.

He was halfway down the trail. Coralee had seen him. Color sprang into her pale face. She twisted around, looking at him fully, the plaits of yellow hair whipping across her shoulders.

And in that moment he saw that he was discovered, because Kilhaven's gun swept up. And sunlight touched the weapon in Hake's hand. An instant choice of targets had to be made, and Con chose the nearest, Kilhaven. But the hammer under his stiffened thumb dropped too late. He felt a slashing pain explode in his right thigh. Flashing of sky above him suddenly, and then below him. He came up, rolling at the bottom of the trail. The instinct gained from a lifetime on this frontier, gained from the war enabled him to be firing the gun even before he halted his downward plunge. Kilhaven, a hand to his bleeding face, sprawled loosely on the ground.

Hake was sprinting toward Coralee, trying to seize her for a shield. But Con drove a bullet between them. Hake leaped back, steadied himself for surer aim. Con struggled up, weight on his left leg. His right numbed and wet.

A wicked orange eye winked at him and he jerked his head aside. Another flashing fire, this time across his neck. Desperately he tried to remember how many shots were left in the revolver. *How many!*

The aching thumb drew back the hammer, let it fall. Drew it back, let it fall. And then it was clicking, the crashing roar of gunfire gone. Hake lay on his side, his eyes sick.

"You fool you," he gasped. "You could have had so much. Now you have nothing. Why didn't you listen to Arch—"

He fell over on his face, and there was a sharp snapping sound as the weight of his lifeless body crushed down on a twisted arm.

"Con, Con, you're hurt," Coralee breathed, and tried to tear at the bonds that held her wrists. They would not give.

He felt sick but he tried to smile at her. "We're in a fix. I've got no knife to cut you loose."

He found himself on his back, the sun in his eyes. Coralee's voice was pleading with him to get up. She knelt beside him, helpless with her bound hands. He dragged himself across the ground. Hake's pockets revealed nothing. But on the dead Kilhaven he found a small ivory-handled clasp knife. He freed Coralee.

Instantly she went to work, tearing the dead Hake's shirt off. She used this as a bandage for his thigh. The wound on his neck was a scratch, he said. But it pained.

"You wanted to see Arizona," he said, his voice faltering. "So do I. Will you go there and wait? I'll drive my cows—" a faint smile touched his lips as he thought of the stiff-backed ex-major. "My group of cows."

She pressed her warm mouth against his, then drew back,

her eyes worried. "You'll need nursing. I won't be the first woman to go on a cattle drive."

"I suppose, to save your reputation, I should marry you."

"It's not a thing to jest about."

"No, you're right." He looked over at the dead Hake, stripped of his shirt, torso gleaming in the sun. He thought of all this man had cost the Bend in lives, in unhappiness. "I sometimes wonder if I'll ever find anything to jest about again."

"You will," she whispered, and kissed him again. "Everything passes in time."

"But not this," he said, suddenly holding her fiercely. "Don't let this pass—ever."

And after a moment she said huskily, "You're supposed to be a sick man. I'll get the horses. I think we'd better find somebody to marry us—"

"I gave my word to Yankees that I'd protect their interests. And I did, as long as possible. I give you my word to marry you."

"Are you in pain?" she whispered.

"Not now." But it was only a partial lie.